## Help me!

*"Can you talk, Kelley?"*

*"That's okay. Don't try anymore. We have to run a tube so you can breathe."*

*"I'm here, honey, Mommy's here . . ."*

*Why isn't she holding my hand? Where is my hand? . . . I can't breathe . . . Dear God, what do I do? All these people with gloves and masks and all I can see are eyes . . .*

*"Kelley. Kelley, can you hear me? My name is Leslie. I'm a nurse. I want you to look at me. That's a girl. I'm going to be taking care of you, hon . . ."*

*"The swelling has started. Intubation. Have you got it?"*

*"Some pins. We need to hold this leg together."*

*"It's deep. Look at the face."*

*I tried to be a good person all my life. I love you, Mom and Leah. I love you EO and Tigger. Please, God, take care of them.*

*"Definitely some third degree here. The other eye's closing, too . . ."*

*The light is going out . . . so sleepy . . . My God, so this is what it's like . . .*

*"Kelley, my name is Leslie. Take a good look at me, Kelley, because you won't be seeing me for a while."*

---

# OTHER PUFFIN BOOKS YOU MAY ENJOY

# a
# face
# first

*Priscilla*
*Cummings*

**PUFFIN BOOKS**

*For Hannah*

PUFFIN BOOKS
Published by the Penguin Group
Penguin Putnam Books for Young Readers,
345 Hudson Street, New York, New York 10014, U.S.A.
Penguin Books Ltd, 80 Strand, London WC2R ORL, England
Penguin Books Australia Ltd,
250 Camberwell Road, Camberwell, Victoria 3124, Australia
Penguin Books Canada Ltd, 10 Alcorn Avenue, Toronto, Ontario, Canada M4V 3B2
Penguin Books (N.Z.) Ltd, 182-190 Wairau Road, Auckland 10, New Zealand

Penguin Books Ltd, Registered Offices: Harmondsworth, Middlesex, England

First published in the United States of America by Dutton Children's Books,
a division of Penguin Putnam Books for Young Readers, 2001
Published by Puffin Books,
a division of Penguin Putnam Books for Young Readers, 2003

3  5  7  9  10  8  6  4  2

THE LIBRARY OF CONGRESS HAS CATALOGED THE DUTTON EDITION AS FOLLOWS:
A Face First / Priscilla Cummings, date.—1st ed.
p.  cm..
Summary: Twelve-year-old Kelley decides to shut off contact with her friends
and classmates after suffering third-degree burns to her face and body
in a car accident near her home on Maryland's Kent Island.
ISBN 0-525-46522-7
[1.Burns and scalds—Fiction. 2. Maryland—Fiction.] I. Title.
PZ7.C9149 Fac 2001
[Fic]—dc21  00-04420

Puffin Books ISBN 0-14-230247-3
Printed in the United States of America

# Acknowledgments

I WISH TO ACKNOWLEDGE the generous help of many patients and staff members at the Baltimore Regional Burn Center at Johns Hopkins Bayview Medical Center in Baltimore, Maryland, especially Lana Parsons and Ceal Curry. I also want to thank Dr. Samuel Libber; Kathryn Marchi; Malcolm, Merrill, Lindsay, and Les Foster; and Maryland's Department of Natural Resources.

A special "thank you" to one incredible woman, LaWanda Conaway, for sharing her story and her inspiration.

From long ago, my thanks to Dr. Andrew Munster, Nancy Green, Ellen Ungar, Leslie Tudahl, and Stan Heuisler.

And finally, to Kathleen Eckelt, wherever she may be, my heartfelt thanks and this:

*Kathleen, we met briefly, many years ago. You were a nurse then, remembering for me, and I have never forgotten.*

*God, give us grace to accept with serenity the things that cannot be changed, courage to change the things which should be changed, and the wisdom to distinguish the one from the other.*

—REINHOLD NIEBUHR

a

face

first

*one*

THE DAY OF THE ACCIDENT Kelley got up early to paint the world on her left thumbnail. It was late April, early spring, and the cool morning air seeping through Kelley's partially opened window carried reminders of a freshly turned field beyond the pasture where her pony grazed. If she had stopped a moment to kneel on the striped cushion of her window seat and look out toward the cove, Kelley would have seen the first pink and orange fingers of dawn gently lifting the heavy night sky. She would have heard the great blue heron shrilly announcing his presence as he did every morning down on the dock. A few seconds, and Kelley could have had this small slice of home to take with her. But there was no way for her to know, and in her haste, she rushed by the window, slamming it shut, then grabbed the basket of nail polish from atop her bureau to take downstairs.

That day, the sixth grade was planting a dogwood tree in recognition of Earth Day, and Kelley had been chosen to read part of the dedication. She had an oversize index card with notes carefully printed on it so that when she spoke into the portable microphone she wouldn't stutter or go "ummm" trying to remember what to say. Mrs. Fox, the school principal, told Kelley they would stand together beneath the flagpole.

It made Kelley nervous to think that, while she spoke, everyone in school would be staring at her, scrutinizing her clothes, her face, her hair, her hands. And so, last night, Kelley had painted each of her fingernails with green nail polish. Not a neon green or anything gaudy like that, just an earthy garden green—for Earth Day—a green that matched her tiny, shiny frog earrings and the headband, socks, and T-shirt she was wearing with her suspender jeans.

Of course her two best friends, Liesel and Alison, were painting their fingernails green, too. It was Alison's idea in the first place. But the idea for painting the world on her left thumbnail was Kelley's alone—an inspiration that came at two o'clock in the morning, just after Tigger had awakened her with a start by knocking the water glass off her nightstand.

"Bad cat," Kelley had groaned, snapping on the light by her bed. Tigger jumped onto the windowsill and looked at her reproachfully, the way cats do. Sleepily, Kelley had plucked a wad of Kleenex from its container. As she began to sop up the damage, her fresh green fingernails surprised her. They reminded her of her speech and what she would be saying about the sixth-grade project— how she and Daniel, Eric, and Melissa had installed chicken wire on the roof of the Islander Hardware Store to prevent the baby terns from falling off after they were hatched.

"They're losing their natural habitat because of waterfront development," Kelley planned to tell her audience, lifting her eyes a moment, to let it sink in. "A big, flat roof looks like a beach to them. It's just that they don't know about the edges." There was something else in her notes about everyone doing his or her bit. "Each of us *can* make this world a little better. . . ." And suddenly Kelley had the cool idea of painting the whole world on her left thumbnail.

Now, sitting at the kitchen table surrounded by a heap of paper towels, cotton balls, and small containers of nail polish, Kelley repainted the thumbnail blue—for the oceans—then painstakingly applied the outlines of the continents with the delicate, pointed tip of her thinnest applicator. The edges were the most difficult. But it was crucial, as she had discovered with the young terns; you had to establish the edges first—or you'd spill over.

The automatic coffeemaker clicked itself on, and Kelley heard the faucet run upstairs, the first sign that her mother was awake. Kelley glanced at the clock on the kitchen stove: six o'clock. No one could ever say her mother wasn't punctual, Kelley thought. She *had* to be. They both had to be because there was so much to do in the morning before leaving, and they needed to be all the way over the bridge and in Annapolis for school by 8:15.

It was just Kelley and her mom now that Leah, Kelley's sister, was off at college, this year studying in Paris. Kelley finished painting in Western Europe with three minuscule dabs of her brush. Leah was in that fresh wet dot of green polish right now, Kelley thought. Quickly, she did the calculations. Paris was six hours ahead of Maryland, so it would be lunchtime over there. Kelley envisioned her sister in sunglasses, her long blond hair pinned up in a sophisticated way, sitting at a sidewalk café with a backpack full of interesting books slung over the back of her chair. Two or three friends were leaning toward her, all of them laughing, as they ordered in French—*bien sûr!*—some bread, some cheese, some wine maybe? Oh, and the waiter—the waiter would be falling in love with Leah, the way everyone did.

Kelley sighed wistfully. The house was so quiet, so empty without Leah. And to think she had once looked forward to that. Kelley focused back on the fingernail. She did not want to dwell on her sister. Quickly, she painted in Africa and Asia. She was glad when her mother shuffled in, flicking on more lights and rubbing her arms to get warm.

"Morning, Mom," Kelley greeted her.

"Ummm. You're up early," her mother said, squinting from the overhead light. She came closer to get a better look at the fingernail project and slowly shook her head. But from the corner of her eye, Kelley could see her mother's mouth lifting at the corners.

"You're a hot ticket, Kel," her mother said into her ear.

Pleased, Kelley scrunched up her shoulders, enjoying the feel of her mother's hands as they gently lifted Kelley's shoulder-length brown hair from where it had fallen inside her bathrobe and smoothed it out over the collar.

The coffeemaker finished its brewing with a hiss, and Kelley's mother moved off to the cabinet to get a mug.

"There. All done!" Kelley announced. She blew softly on the finished nail. "Pretty good, huh?" She stuck her thumb up in the air for approval.

"It's cute."

Kelley blew on her thumbnail some more.

*The sheen of fresh nail polish.*

*"You're a hot ticket, Kel. . . ."*

*The smell of her mother's coffee.*

Kelley would remember the ordinary details of this morning with an uncanny clarity.


Only one thing happened that morning that could be considered a premonition: the telephone call with no one at the other end. This wouldn't have seemed so strange except that it had happened two days in a row. For a split second, Kelley held the receiver and wondered if someone was trying to scope out their house.

"No one there?" her mother asked.

Kelley hung up and shook her head.

"Don't worry about it, then." Her mother folded up the newspaper she'd been reading. "Look. I'm going upstairs to exercise, then I'm jumping in the shower."

"Okay," Kelley replied, distracted. "I'll change and go feed the horses."

Her mother pushed her chair in and left the room.

Kelley tried to finish eating but couldn't and ended up putting the rest of her oatmeal in the sink. She wondered if it was that horror movie Liesel rented last weekend— the one where this creepy guy spied on a family for a whole week and then . . . Kelley shuddered, not wanting to recall the story.

On the way upstairs to change, Kelley heard her mother pounding away on the wooden slats of her NordicTrack. Through the partly opened door, Kelley could see her mother's arms and legs moving back and forth with great determination while she watched the morning news on a small television set.

In her room, Kelley pulled on her barn clothes: old blue jeans and a sweatshirt. She picked up her backpack and brought it downstairs to set by the kitchen door. But everywhere she went the phone call followed her. She couldn't shake the lingering anxiety it had left behind. Walking across the yard to the barn, she turned her head from side to side to see if anyone was watching.

Tigger was with her then, trotting ahead with his tail in the air, meowing when it took her too long to open the door. He always came with her to do the chores, checked out all his favorite places, then stepped onto Kelley's back from the ladder to the hayloft while she was bent over scooping grain from a burlap sack into two metal buckets. He rubbed his furry head against the back of Kelley's neck and then jumped back onto the ladder when she straightened up.

A large gray horse in the stall behind Kelley snorted impatiently and began stomping one of his heavy front hooves. "I'm coming, Pulsar, I'm *coming*," Kelley said, hoisting one of the buckets.

The horse moved his big head up and down as Kelley entered his stall and plunged into the grain before she had even set the bucket on the floor. "Calm down," Kelley said, stroking the powerful neck beneath his black mane. Pulsar belonged to Julianna, an old friend of Leah's, who boarded him at the Brennans. Julianna would come to let her horse and Kelley's pony out later. Kelley patted the tall gelding once more on his strong, high withers. "Behave yourself now," she said.

Kelley took the other grain bucket to her pony, EO, who stood with his head hanging, in the next stall. He was an old pony—he'd been Leah's long before he was Kelley's—and Kelley wondered now if he was losing his hearing.

"Hey!" she called from the open doorway. "You awake?"

Sleepily, the pony swung his head around. Kelley set the bucket down in front of him and lifted his shaggy forelock, straightening it so she could see his big brown eyes. Practically all of her allowance went toward EO's up-keep.

"Time to rise and shine," she said.

EO's nostrils perked up, and he issued a short, low whinny. Kelley cupped his fuzzy ears in her hands and kissed the soft white star on his forehead. Then carefully, so as not to smudge her fresh nail polish, Kelley reached into her pocket for the handful of Froot Loops EO loved.

"Here you go," she said, holding her hand flat as he worked his wide velvet muzzle to sweep the cereal off her hand. When he was through, Kelley hugged him around the neck and lifted the grain bucket up to EO's nose so she was sure he knew it was there.

While the animals ate their grain, Kelley threw them each several squares of hay and then filled two more buckets with water from a spigot near the front of the barn. The buckets were heavy, and some of the water sloshed over the edges as she carried it across the cement floor. Finally, she double-checked the latches on both of the stall doors, called Tigger, and closed up the barn.

By then, she had stopped thinking about the telephone call. Only later, in a crazed and fitful search for meaning, would she wonder if it was some sort of a celestial warning.

"Come *on,* we've got to go," her mother insisted, rattling her keys, rolling her eyes, tapping her shoe as Kelley rushed from room to room hunting for her white sneakers. A former secretary, Kelley's mother had just finished a series of night classes and was now a real-estate agent. But she was new at the job and liked getting into the office early every day.

Finally, Kelley spotted the sneakers behind the magazine rack. She had thrown them there when she vacuumed the rug, after she spilled popcorn.

A sigh of relief. A mad dash out of the house. A slamming door. Silence in the car as her mother sped down the road with two hands on the steering wheel. Kelley turned to look out the side window and catch her breath. In her head, she practiced the end of her speech: "Why should we care about the least tern? It's just a little bird, smoky gray with a white belly and a tiny black cap. I held one in the palm of my hand last year. . . . We in Maryland should *care* because this little bird has a right to live and its existence is threatened."

Up ahead, Kelley noticed how the morning sun gilded the gathering storm clouds. She hoped it wasn't going to rain. Rain would spoil the dedication ceremony.

Her mother leaned forward to look behind in the side-view mirror. The turn signal was on—*click, click, click*—as she merged the car into a stream of traffic and sped away from Kent Island heading west, across the four-mile bridge that spanned the Chesapeake Bay.


"All eyes up here!" Mr. Canone, her science teacher, tapped the blackboard with his pointer. But he had just said something that made Kelley laugh and she couldn't, just then, pay attention. She figured this must have been after lunch, after the dedication ceremony, because science was sixth period on Wednesday. They were studying cells, amoebas. Kelley couldn't remember what was so funny, but she covered her mouth to laugh, and Daniel, catching her eye, laughed with her.

Then what happened?

Memories of that afternoon grew sketchy, Kelley discovered later, after the accident, when she tried to piece it all together. She remembered part of the ride home, on Route 50, after ballet. She and her mother talked about school. Her mother always wanted to know how the day went. Kelley could still see her mother handing the token at the bridge, dropping it as she did because she was in a rush, and commenting as the window went up: "It's starting to rain."

But was Kelley's hair up from ballet class? Did she and her mother eat out that night? Sometimes, they went to the food court at the mall and Kelley ordered Chinese, some pork fried rice, and started her homework while her mother ate a salad and worked on her lists of things to do.

At first, Kelley did not remember anything at all about what happened at the intersection. She knew where the exit off Route 50 met Route 8 because she and her mother went through it every day on their way home. There was a sign on the approach with arrows pointing left to Stevensville and right to Romancoke, a traffic signal overhead where the two-lane road met.

But there was no recollection of a speeding truck. No echoes from the explosion, nor a single splinter of the many sounds that surely would have lingered like recurring aftershocks: the shatter of breaking glass, the crunch of heavy metal, the blare from a stuck horn.

Perhaps most mercifully of all, Kelley would think later, there was no recall whatsoever of a fire so hot, and so close, it melted the shape from a small frog earring.

Over time, other things would come back, briefly, and often at random. But they were mere snatches of memory with ragged, open edges that appeared from out of nowhere, like sentences from a paragraph that has been cut up and dropped into a bag from which someone plucks them, one at a time, to read aloud, hauntingly, when no one but Kelley is listening. . . .

*"Can you talk, Kelley?"*

*"That's okay. Don't try anymore. We have to run a tube so you can breathe."*

*"I'm here, honey, Mommy's here . . ."*

*Why isn't she holding my hand? Where is my hand? . . . I can't breathe . . . Dear God, what do I do? All these people with gloves and masks and all I can see are eyes . . .*

*"Kelley. Kelley, can you hear me? My name is Leslie. I'm a nurse. I want you to look at me. That's a girl. I'm going to be taking care of you, hon . . ."*

*"The swelling has started. Intubation. Have you got it?"*

*"Some pins. We need to hold this leg together."*

*"It's deep. Look at the face."*

*I tried to be a good person all my life. I love you, Mom and*

Leah. I love you, EO and Tigger. Please, God, take care of them.

"Definitely some third degree here. The other eye's closing, too . . ."

The light is going out . . . so sleepy . . . My God, so this is what it's like . . .

"Kelley, my name is Leslie. Take a good look at me, Kelley, because you won't be seeing me for a while."

# two

THE DAYS THAT FOLLOWED BLURRED together like a dream. Day was night and night was day, and it didn't matter. Everything was dark. Moments of abject pain melded with long, drug-induced naps and fragmented visions. Kelley couldn't seem to get warm. And conversations drifted in and out, from near and far.

"The blood pressure is good . . . finally stabilized . . ." "Dr. Brewer said to go ahead, then . . ." "Concern for the right hand, here to here . . ." "I slept in the waiting room . . ."

*Mommy! Where are you? . . .*

"There is a cafeteria, you know . . ." "Maybe just some coffee . . ." "Prep for the OR, then . . . No, leave the splint on the left hand . . ." "They serve breakfast until really late, eleven, I think . . ." "She's trembling . . . is that normal?" . . . "A read on the vitals, please . . ."

*It hurts, Mommy, it hurts . . .*

"Someone, look! She's biting the tube!" "Let's have a check here . . . Give me a morphine level . . ."

*Mommy!*

"It's all right . . . go to sleep now."

Kelley wondered, more than once, if she had died and gone to heaven. But she was too weak, too tired to probe her feelings about it. Then the pain would start again, and she knew she was alive. Alive and often astonishingly aware of what was going on.

Even when her eyes were still swollen shut, there were crystallized, surreal moments when, mentally, Kelley could step outside of herself to see the sterile cocoon of technology that was keeping her alive. The narrow plastic tubes that came and went, giving and taking. The delicate wires taped to her body that measured every heartbeat, every breath she took in colorful blipping lines that raced with importance across a monitor over her left shoulder. The body-length heat cradle that hovered above her, like a guardian angel, trying to keep her warm.

*I'm so cold, so cold, so cold . . .*

"Kelley, Dr. Brewer here . . . surgery on your hand . . . doing fine . . ."

*Medicine smells. Everywhere . . .*

"It's Mom . . . Can she hear me? Do you think she can hear me?"

*Mommy, yes! I can hear you!*

"To explain what's happening . . ." "Surgically removed skin from the back of the left leg . . . a graft . . . to prevent infection . . ." "Tell her that's why her thigh hurts . . ."

*I can't see . . . God, why can't I see? I'm so scared . . .*

"I need help with the IV . . . can you keep that leg up?"

*If I wake up, will I see you?*

"I'll be back then . . . Kelley, it's okay, sweetie . . ."

*No—no, it's not okay! Don't leave me!*

Through it all, like a thin, dark thread linking everything, came a man's voice, crying. Even through the long tunnels of silence, Kelley could hear his solitary wail. When the tube in her throat was finally out—someone said it was there for three days—Kelley kept swallowing and asking in a hoarse, urgent whisper, "Who is it?"

But no one understood her. They all leaned close to hear and thought she wanted to know who was there, by her bed, so they answered, "It's Mom" or "I'm Leslie" or, in his clipped German accent, "Dr. Brewer come to check."

And Kelley would forget about the man crying and ask instead, "Are my fingers there?" because her hand was partly numb, and she still couldn't see.

"Every single one!" Leslie said brightly, lifting Kelley's hand and tapping the tip of each gauze-wrapped digit.

Leslie even teased her about the green nail polish, so Kelley knew she was telling the truth. It's just that nothing registered. Nothing stuck. She felt adrift without an anchor. Words, sounds, smells—everything mingled and surrounded her, flooding the cavity she floated in, then disappeared, collected and came again, like waves washing over her.

"I'm so cold," Kelley whispered, because it still hurt to talk. Someone put a hand on hers.

"Here's an extra blanket, okay? There. How's that?"

The blanket was warm. It felt as though it had just come out of the oven. Kelley mouthed a silent "Thank you."

"It's Anita, Kelley. I'm a physical therapist." She spoke slowly. "I'm here to exercise your hands a little so they won't get stiff. I want you to relax as much as you can."

Anita's voice was kind. Kelley imagined Anita was very pretty. Kelley tried to say "okay," but it came out a meek " 'kay."

Gently, Anita removed the splint and bandages from Kelley's right hand. "The graft you just had looks great, Kelley. Lots of little pink buds. And *that* is the first sign of new skin."

Little pink buds. New skin. In her mind, Kelley envisioned a flower garden sprouting hands instead of blossoms. It was kind of gross, though. She groaned.

"I'm sorry. Did that hurt?" Anita asked.

Kelley moved her head to say no, but stiffened when Anita began touching the unprotected wounds on her hand. One by one, the therapist forced each of Kelley's fingers to move slowly, back and forth. The pressure hurt. The movement hurt. Everything hurt.

Kelley began to breathe hard. She just wanted Anita to go away and let her sleep.


"It's Tuesday, May fourth," Leslie said as she laid out her gauze and Q-tips and prepared for the daily dressings. Kelley could feel these things being placed on the sheet that covered her stomach and her left leg. The swelling on her face had just started to retreat, and she was able, with one uncovered eye, to make out hazy, amorphous outlines. She thought she could see her broken right leg propped up on the bed in front of her and a white form hunched over it, peeling away dead skin from the burn.

May 4. The date echoed in Kelley's head.

"You've been here almost a week," Leslie told her.

Kelley was still stuck on the date. If this was May 4, then she had missed the May Day Dance at school. She didn't get to wear her new outfit. She had a new outfit, didn't she?

May 4. Now she remembered. There was a test today. A test on the China unit in history. She had outlined with a red pen the entire May 4 page in her assignment book.

"Kelley Brennan, you have the most wonderful mother in the world," Leslie went on. "Do you know that? She brought you a huge bouquet of purple lilacs this morning. They are so pretty. And they smell good, too. She says she got them from a bush in your backyard."

Kelley's mind drifted. She tried to smile at the thought of home, of the garden on the hill behind the house where her mother would have picked those lilacs, but she was sure her mouth barely twitched. She tried to see her hands and wondered why she could feel one and not the other and then grunted a little in frustration, something that sounded like "uh," to keep Leslie talking. When there was someone talking it was easier to focus away from the pain. Plus she liked the sound of Leslie's husky, almost masculine voice. She found comfort in the fact that it never changed, never wavered, not even when the pain became so bad that Kelley started to cry or scream.

It got so Kelley knew the smell of Leslie's perfume so well she could tell when the nurse was on duty before Leslie even came near the bed or spoke a single word.

"What kind?" Kelley asked.

"What kind of what?" Leslie was focused on the leg and had painstakingly gripped another sliver of burned skin with the tweezers.

Kelley began to tense up. "Perfume," she struggled to say. She tried so hard to be brave. "Kind of perfume . . . do you wear?"

"Oh—it's Tuscany," Leslie replied with a chuckle. She removed the skin and wiped off the tweezers. "Every year on our anniversary my husband, Joe, takes me to Tio Pepe's for dinner and gives me a big spray bottle of Tuscany. It's a tradition!

"Then, listen to this, Kelley. My son, Adam, who's ten, saves up and gets me the little bottle for Christmas. He's done this the last two years, and it breaks me up because an ounce of that stuff costs thirty-seven dollars!"

The man started to cry again. His voice was a high-pitched needle that intruded and picked at their own conversation. Kelley tried to figure out where the voice came from. Her room? Across the hall? Was this man a patient? Or a father? *Her* father?

Kelley thought she heard her father once. *Hey, Kel. How ya doin'?* Thought she felt his presence close to her face. Kelley longed for her father at the strangest times. Did someone call him? Could he get here from California that fast?

"How long have I . . . been here?" Kelley asked.

"Almost a week," Leslie repeated. She repositioned a tub of warm water on the bed and was zeroing in with the tweezers when the man cried out again. Suddenly, Kelley panicked. *His* pain and *her* pain had become one horrible, ripping sensation that no amount of morphine could mask.

"Stop!" she screamed, pressing herself against the bed with such a jolt that Leslie had to grab the pan of water before it spilled.

"Whoa! Hold on!" Leslie moved the water onto the floor and held Kelley's shoulders down, to keep her still. "It's okay, hon. Let it out. We'll take a break. Go ahead and cry. Go ahead, I know it hurts. I know it does."

It was a pain worse than anything Kelley had ever known. A pain with no end to it! No mercy!

"Relax now," Leslie said calmly. "Take in a full breath and let it out slow."

Kelley inhaled deeply but exhaled too fast and had to

start over. She could still hear the man, who was whimpering like an unhappy puppy.

Kelley let her breath out slowly this time. "The man crying," she said. It was still hard to talk because she couldn't open her mouth very far.

"Yes. The man crying. What about him?" Leslie waited.

"He my father?"

"Gosh, Kelley, no," Leslie said.

This didn't surprise Kelley, and it didn't disappoint her. In fact, Kelley tried to picture what her father looked like right then and couldn't do it.

"Your father called you, though. And he sent you a huge stuffed Dalmatian. I'm looking at him right now. He's sitting over there in the corner with a bright green collar and his big red tongue hanging out."

Kelley sort of half heard all this. Her father. A phone call. A big dog in the corner. Why a dog? Kelley didn't much like dogs. But he probably didn't know that.

The man cried again.

"Who is it, then?" Kelley asked.

"That's Leonard across the hall," Leslie said.

"Leonard?"

"Uh-huh. His name is Leonard."

"Why's he crying?"

"Why's he crying? Because he hurts," Leslie answered. "Like you."

"He's burned?"

Sometimes Leslie had to stop what she was doing and

lean in really close to hear what Kelley was saying or asking.

"Yes, he's burned," she said. "Everyone on this floor has a burn, Kelley. That's why you're here. This is a special burn unit in a Baltimore hospital."

Kelley knew this. She had forgotten it, though. "He worse?" she asked. "He worse than me?"

"Everyone in here suffers, Kelley. Whether it's a small burn or a big burn. But if you added everything up, then, yes, I suppose so. Leonard is worse off than you. He was burned in a house fire a month ago. Fell asleep smoking a cigarette. He burned his own house down and lost an arm and a leg doing it."

Kelley tried to imagine this.

"Do you know why he's crying?" Leslie asked her.

Kelley barely moved her head against the pillow. "He's sad?"

"Yes. He's sad. He's sad because he hurts, and we're making him eat a canned pear this morning. All by himself. You see, the arm we saved was still burned so badly that he needs to teach the mending muscles all over again how to do their work. Rehabilitation, they call it. You'll need some, too. Hasn't Anita already been in to exercise your hands?"

Kelley tried but could barely wiggle the fingers of her hands, both of which lay taped up and in splints at her side.

"Your leg especially will need a lot of exercise after the fracture has healed," Leslie said.

Kelley peered down at the leg Leslie had been working on. She knew there were pins holding the shattered bone together. Pins because they couldn't put a cast over burned skin that hadn't healed. Kelley tried to move her leg once and saw how the long silver pins protruded from one side like six, evenly spaced skewers in a giant shish kebab. She shuddered, unable to remember how long they would be there.

"Your mouth, too, Kelley. You know how hard it is for you to talk?"

Kelley tried to nod.

"It's because the burn on your face extends to the corner of your mouth. I want you to understand this," Leslie said. "So it's not so much of a shock later."

"But I *don't* understand," Kelley complained weakly. "If my face was burned so badly . . . then why doesn't it hurt *more?*" She took a breath. "Like my leg? And my hands?"

"Because it's all a third-degree burn, Kelley. The face burn is more extensive and deeper than your other burns. Your hands, your leg—a lot of the skin there was burned second degree, not just third. A third-degree burn destroys all your sweat glands, all your hair follicles—*and* the nerve endings. Do you see? That's why you don't feel the pain in your face."

No nerve endings. No pain. If Leslie had told her that, she had forgotten.

"On your face, new skin is never going to grow back on its own," Leslie explained further, watching her closely.

"That is why, in a couple weeks, Kelley, they'll do a skin graft there. Same thing they did on your right hand. Same thing they'll do on part of that leg after the bone heals up."

She paused. "You okay?"

Kelley could feel the tears pooling.

"Hey! But you're lucky," Leslie said, lightly grasping her forearms.

Kelley stared in her direction with a watery, disbelieving eye.

"You won't have to start from scratch like Leonard. He has to relearn how to pick up a spoon. How to get a piece of pear onto the spoon. How to lift the spoon to his mouth. And *then* how to open his mouth wide enough to get the spoon and the pear inside without dropping them!

"It is such a monumental task for him, Kelley, that sometimes he gets frustrated." Leslie screwed up her face. "*Really frustrated.* He can taste his own sweat. And he cries. He doesn't stop trying, though. He just keeps crying while he struggles with that spoon.

"But I want to tell you something. Leonard is his own miracle. No one on the burn unit thought he would ever make it this far. He reached inside and found a strength that would not quit. A few more weeks and I think he'll go home.

"You will, too, Kelley," she said.

They sat quietly for a few seconds. Maybe it was longer. There was no way for Kelley to know for sure. It seemed, and didn't seem, like a long time.

"Now listen," Leslie said in her calm, measured voice. "I want you to put all of your worries aside right now. Stuff 'em in a bottle, okay? Put the stopper in—nice and tight. That's a girl. Set the bottle on a shelf. Good! Now—walk away and think of one of your happiest memories."

Right away Kelley thought of the snowstorm.

"No school," Kelley struggled to say, "because of snow." But she simply didn't have the energy to tell Leslie how for three days she and her family had been snowed in. "Leah," Kelley added, because Leah was there, too.

Gently, Leslie prodded. "And your mom and dad?"

Kelley paused because, of course, her father wasn't there. In fact, she had no memory of ever living with her father because he had left so long ago.

"Mom was home," she whispered. Her mother worked as a receptionist for a dentist then, but the dentist had closed his office because of the weather. Leah and Kelley cheered and threw the couch pillows into the air! Their mother made hot chocolate with marshmallows. She set up a card table in front of the fireplace, and they put together a huge jigsaw puzzle. It was a seaport scene in Mystic, Connecticut. Kelley remembered a pot of red geraniums on the cobblestone walk, a weather vane shaped like a whale.

"Monopoly," Kelley said because they had played Monopoly, too. One night, when the electricity was off, they curled up in sleeping bags downstairs by the fire to finish a game by candlelight. Tigger was just a kitten. He crouched in the cover of the Monopoly box and batted the tiny houses with his paws.

"There's a Monopoly game down in the playroom. Would you like me to get it out sometime?" Leslie asked.

"Ummm," Kelley said sleepily.

"I've got to warn you, though, I'm pretty stiff competition."

"Tired," Kelley said.

"Okay. Go to sleep, hon. But what I want you to remember, Kelley, is that you are going to get better and walk on out of here."

Kelley tried to nod and, as she began to slip into sleep, she imagined herself walking into the Annapolis mall one afternoon with Alison and Liesel. They were giggling as they stepped up to a cosmetic counter at Nordstrom's. Kelley asked for the biggest bottle of Tuscany they had and wrote on a little gold card: *For Leslie, who saw me through a hard time.*

It was one of many fragmented visions Kelley had in those first days, when dreaming was the only refuge from the pain and torment of reality. But one thing about those dreams early on is that they kept her going through the worst of it because they all had hope. They were all linked to a normal life; like walking into the mall to buy perfume and knowing that her fingers were still there—graced with green nail polish.

What Kelley couldn't see yet was that on the left thumbnail, the world had melted off.

# three

WHEN THE SWELLING ON HER face finally went down and when there wasn't too much lubricant in her eyes smearing her vision, Kelley could see all the way down the Patapsco River to the Francis Scott Key Bridge. Although it was miles away, the bridge loomed high and prominent against the eastern sky. It was the first thing Kelley looked for every day, because she knew that just beyond the bridge, the river emptied into the Chesapeake Bay and that across the bay, on Kent Island, home waited for her.

No patient had ever asked before, but Kelley begged them until finally they turned her bed around so she could look out that window all the time. Because even when fog or rain obscured her view of the bridge, Kelley could watch the stream of traffic moving up and down Eastern Avenue.

The traffic never stopped. At two, three—four o'clock in the morning, headlights came and went steadily in the darkness. Like a pulse, Kelley couldn't help but think. Life outside the hospital went on: People got in their cars, buckled themselves in, and went places, even if it was just to pick up shirts at the cleaners or get a gallon of milk at the 7-Eleven or order a meatball sub at Jerry's.

Eastern Avenue also brought her mother, every day, around 7:00 P.M., when Baltimore's rush hour was winding down. Her mother had a different car, of course, but Kelley still looked for a yellow station wagon to come in from the left, where there was an exit off the interstate.

"Hey, there!" her mother said cheerfully, coming into the room with a smile despite the huge bruise over her left eye. "Look what I brought!"

Kelley watched her lift a huge bouquet of pink roses from the bag she carried.

"To celebrate the end of Week One," her mother said. She didn't wait for a response from Kelley. "And that's not all. I've got letters from Alison and Liesel, your favorite pillow—oh, and one more little thing."

Kelley had to smile, if even wanly, at the sight of her plush panda, the one Leah won for her at Rehoboth Beach years ago. She reached for him, and her mother settled him in her arms.

Her mother always came bearing gifts. If it wasn't roses, it was a bunch of yellow daffodils, a new book, or a compact disc that Kelley could listen to with earphones on her new portable CD player. There were also notes and cards from classmates, as well as other familiar items from home—her worn wooden hairbrush, the clock radio from her night table, her red-checkered nightshirt.

All of these things came in a large canvas bag that Kelley's mother carried in one hand. One hand because the other hand had been burned in the accident, too, and was heavily bandaged. Besides the facial bruise, there was a cut below her mother's knee that required eight stitches. The air bag, they said, had prevented more terrible things from happening to her.

It was an old car and there wasn't an air bag on the passenger side, just a seat belt, which Kelley had buckled, as she always did. But most everyone agreed that an air bag wouldn't have prevented Kelley's injuries anyway because of the fire and the way the engine tore through the side of the car where she was sitting.

It gave Kelley a stomachache each time someone mentioned one of these things or started talking about the accident. It was hard to figure, but she felt as though they were rooting around in a delicate area.

In her own mind, Kelley erected a wall to prevent herself from looking backward. She imagined this wall to be twice her height and made of brick. The wall became such a real fixture in her mind that Kelley even told the policeman who had come to her room that morning that she couldn't remember anything about the accident because it was "behind the wall."

He looked up quizzically, his pen poised, mid-click, over the small notebook in his hand. "I'm sorry?"

Kelley shrugged. "I remember my mother . . . paying

the toll at the bridge. And I remember the rain," she said slowly. "But nothing else. It's behind the wall."

The officer nodded and didn't ask her anything else. He said he had a daughter the same age as Kelley, and Kelley knew he believed her. Kelley felt protected by the wall. She did not need people to chip away at it.

"What I don't understand is where this truck driver was going in such a hurry! What did he say about that?" Kelley's great-aunt Katherine asked later in the evening, when she arrived to visit. She sat on a chair at the foot of Kelley's bed, one hand flailing self-righteously in the air while Kelley's mother listened, humbly, the way people did in Aunt Katherine's presence because she was so loud and so old. No one wanted to be rude to her.

"You know part of the whole problem here is that these truckers think they *own* the roads, so they have their *own* rules. I've seen the way they speed." Aunt Katherine's eyes became enormous. "Lord save us, all the way down on the Pennsylvania Turnpike, that wretched road, they passed me going eighty—ninety miles an hour at least! Now. Imagine *hitting* someone at that speed."

*"Please,"* Kelley piped up weakly.

The two women turned to her.

"Don't talk about what happened," Kelley said. She hugged her panda tightly. "It hurts."

Aunt Katherine put a hand over her ample chest. "God bless, child. I know it must." She looked at Kelley's mother and reached over to touch her hand. "We won't ever mention it again. Will we, Marjorie?"

Kelley's mother shook her head. "No. No, of course not, Kelley. We didn't realize."

Through it all, her mother put up a good front. Kelley knew it was a front, a brave front, because from the moment she could see again, Kelley saw the change in her mother's pale, drawn face and her haunted eyes, red-rimmed with fatigue and worry. Over the next few days, even as the bruise from the accident turned colors and faded, her mother's face never seemed to recover. Kelley noticed lines she had never seen before. Yet her mother never cried, never uttered a single word of despair, never let slip a shard of anger toward the truck driver or anyone else.

"Look! I brought you a big jar of crunchy peanut butter—the kind you like! And one of those little honey bears you squeeze? So you can make a sandwich later!" Her mother held up the little bear hopefully. She had come earlier that day because it was Saturday.

"That's great! Do you like peanut butter?" Leslie asked.

"Yeah, I guess so," Kelley said.

Leslie greeted Kelley's mother, then returned to her task of carefully removing the gauze wrapped around Kelley's face.

Two weeks had passed since the accident, and there were no more bandages on her mother's hand. Kelley noticed that her mother didn't favor it anymore either, and that the blistered, peeling skin was hardly noticeable.

"You like my new top?" her mother asked, holding out her arms to show off a bright yellow cotton shirt with a scoop neck and long sleeves.

"Nice," Kelley murmured.

"Good, 'cause I got one just like it for you!" She pinched Kelley's toe.

Her mother had a new permanent, too; her blond hair fell in soft, perfect ripples around her head, ending in a blunt cut, just below her ears. She had tried gallantly to make a fresh start. But Kelley could still see the new lines in her face, the worry that didn't used to be there.

There was a quiet moment as Leslie finished removing the bandages. Kelley watched her mother's expression. She didn't think her mother had seen her face since the night they brought Kelley into the emergency room. Her mother seemed anxious; she licked her lips and swallowed and slowly put a hand up on her chest. For a split second there was nothing—then, suddenly, her mother burst into a smile.

"Wow!" she exclaimed. Her moist eyes caught Kelley's. "The swelling has really gone down!"

"Hasn't it?" Leslie seemed genuinely pleased.

"I can't believe how far she's come, Leslie. I mean, her voice is so much clearer. And that hand. Look at it." Kelley didn't wear bandages on her hands anymore, only a splint on the right hand.

"That hand *is* looking mighty good," Dr. LaMotte agreed in his deep voice as he entered the room. Dr. LaMotte was the plastic surgeon who would be doing the skin graft on Kelley's face. Kelley thought he was handsome. In fact, she thought he looked a lot like that actor her mother liked so much—Harrison Ford. The guy in all the old *Star Wars* movies.

"I couldn't help but overhear," he said. He shook hands with Kelley's mother. "Good to see you again." Then he flashed a wide grin at Kelley and Leslie. "I just came to take a quick look."

Leslie stepped aside and let Dr. LaMotte take her place.

Everyone was silent as he scrutinized Kelley's face. Suddenly, he made eye contact with Kelley—and winked. "We're gonna fix you up," he said.

Kelley hadn't even realized she was holding her breath until then. She let out a long sigh.

Dr. LaMotte grew serious. "You have to prepare yourself, though. There are going to be several operations, Kelley. Two or three grafts. Some plastic surgery. It's going to take a year—maybe eighteen months before most of it is over. It's possible that more surgery will have to be done three, four years down the road."

*And then what?* Kelley wanted to ask him. *Will I look like myself again?* But a dry sort of ache had settled in her throat, and Kelley couldn't bring herself to say a thing.

Dr. LaMotte touched her wrist. "I'll see you Monday. Get some rest this weekend."

Monday was the first face graft.

After Dr. LaMotte left, Leslie applied ointment to Kelley's face and wrapped clean gauze around and around her head, over her right eye. Kelley imagined sometimes that she must look like half a mummy.

"You two have a nice visit," Leslie said before leaving.

She forgot one of her blue plastic containers of Micropore Paper Surgical Tape. Kelley picked it up in her left hand and touched the sticky side with the only normal fingertip she had on her left hand, her index finger. No one had asked her if *she* wanted to take a look before they sealed her off. Just as well, Kelley thought, because she would have refused.

"I'll get you a fresh ginger ale," her mother said.

Filling time, killing time. After Leslie left, Kelley's mother bustled around as she always did on her visits. Straightaway, she went to the nurses' station to fetch a fresh ginger ale in a tall plastic cup with crushed ice. Then, after reorganizing everything on the bed tray, tacking the newest Get Well cards to the one small bulletin board Kelley had, and plumping the pillows once more, she would reposition the soda and bend the straw toward Kelley. Finally, she would sit down so they could talk for a while.

"I know the pain is awful," her mother sympathized in a soft voice. "God knows, if I could trade places with you I would. But these people are trying to help you, Kelley. The therapist? Anita? She says she understands, but *please, Kelley.* You must never—*ever* hit any of the nurses again."

Kelley looked away. Of course, her mother couldn't understand how it wasn't really *Kelley* who hit the therapist. Kelley was still Kelley inside. It's just that something had happened to Kelley on the outside. It felt as though Anita was ripping her thumb off the way she pushed it backward. Kelley could almost feel the flesh ripping apart. It was instinct! She wasn't totally to blame!

Her mother's canvas bag came next. She pulled out a crossword puzzle book, some root-beer lollipops, and a stack of photographs Leah had sent from Paris. "This is her friend, Mirielle. Cute, isn't she?" her mother asked before catching herself with the "cute" comment. "Leah says she's *very* nice."

When the bag was emptied, Kelley's mother read a couple of news items from the Kent Island page of their local newspaper, then a movie review in *The Baltimore Sun*.

"Do you want help filling out the menu card? Lunch tomorrow is 'Meat Loaf with Gravy' or 'Wellness Teriyaki Chicken'—".

"Mom, stop—I'll do it later."

"Do you want to watch something on TV?"

Kelley shook her head. "I'm sick of it."

"Do you want me to read some more?"

Kelley shrugged.

Her mother looked at her watch.

"I hate to run off," she apologized. "But I've got two people flying in from Ohio early this afternoon. They want to look at property near St. Michael's and they've only got today and tomorrow to do it. So I'm stuck, Kel. You know I've got to work." Her voice pleaded.

"I'll tell Leslie to put the honey and the peanut butter with your other things."

Kelley looked at her.

36

"I love you. You'll be okay tomorrow. I'll be here early Monday morning before the surgery."

The end of her visit had come too soon, Kelley thought. The ends of her visits always came too fast. Only after her mother bent to kiss the top of her head and disappeared out the door did Kelley cry, softly, as she imagined her mother taking the elevator down, leaving the hospital, and getting farther and farther away, until finally she was a tiny speck blending anonymously into the stream of traffic on Eastern Avenue.

Often, Kelley stared at the traffic for a long time after her mother left, wondering where everyone was going. She knew from a nurse that Eastern Avenue went west into Highlandtown, a neighborhood where a great many people lived in old town houses that clung together on steep hills. From her hospital room, Kelley could see their cluttered rooftops and floppy antennae, their white stone steps, and the front porch lights that went on at dusk.

Somewhere in Highlandtown there was a little market called the ABC. Although she had never seen it, she imagined the ABC had a bell over the front door that went *ping!* when you walked in. The nurses encouraged Kelley to order takeout from the ABC if that would get her to eat.

"What do you like?" they asked. But Kelley kept shaking her head weakly because nothing appealed to her.

"Kelley, come on. You've got to eat something," Leslie said to her after Kelley sent away the liver again. But Kelley didn't care how much iron and stuff the liver had. She hadn't liked it to begin with—and they had it twice a week!

"You *need* the extra calories now—two and three times as much," Leslie tried to explain. "Your body is struggling to recuperate and regenerate."

Even if she wasn't hungry, she wished her mother had stayed to make a peanut butter sandwich.

"Do you like milk shakes?" Leslie persisted. "Subs? Hey! How about a grilled cheese with one of those big fat dill pickles from your aunt Katherine?" She had a cotton ball and a bottle of peroxide in her hand and was cleaning the areas on Kelley's right leg where each of six pins protruded from the mending bones in what they called an external fixator. But now Leslie set the cotton and the bottle down, crossed her arms, and studied Kelley's sad expression while Kelley stared at her right hand, stretched open and exposed in front of her.

The splint was off while Kelley exercised the hand and tried to bend all five fingers forward at the first knuckle. Half an inch was her goal. Half an inch, but there was barely any movement at all, her fingers were so stiff and sore. Still, she kept trying, biting her lip and holding back tears.

"That's a girl," Leslie said. "What do you think of that new pink skin? Isn't it beautiful?"

"Yeah, beautiful," Kelley said apathetically. The graft had "taken." Everyone said it looked great. There was even a beautiful, brand-new wrinkle on her right thumb knuckle. But it was at once a wonder and a horror, Kelley

38

thought. A wonder because this was skin from the back of her thigh actually *growing* on her hand; but a horror, too, because the hand was grotesque with its swollen fingers and scabby, discolored flesh.

Leslie thumped the edge of the bed. "Hey! Do you remember telling me about how you and your family played Monopoly during a snowstorm?"

Kelley looked up at her, surprised. "I told you about that?"

Leslie nodded. "Yeah. One day when I was doing the dressings." She raised her eyebrows. "You wouldn't believe some of the stuff you told me."

Kelley didn't catch the wink in Leslie's eye.

"You went on and on about that boy, too. I forget his name."

"Daniel?" Kelley asked timidly.

"Daniel! That's it. *Daniel,*" she said with an exaggerated lilt in her voice.

"You're kidding." She hadn't even confided in Alison and Liesel about her feelings for Daniel. "What did I say?"

Leslie reached down and grabbed Kelley's left ankle through the blanket that covered it. "I am pulling your leg, kid."

Kelley sighed with relief. "I thought so."

"Yeah, sure, you thought so! I'll tell you what. I challenge you to a round of Monopoly *if* you order something incredibly fattening to eat."

Leslie was too much. Kelley *almost* smiled.

"All right," she agreed. "Go ahead. Order us a sausage

and mushroom pizza." She knew that was Leslie's favorite.

It was awkward at first. Kelley had to eat her pizza, drink her chocolate milk shake, and move her game piece around the Monopoly board with her left hand because the right one was back in its splint. But she managed, and was disappointed when they had to put the game aside. "At least I've got Boardwalk," she reminded Leslie.

"Yeah, well, don't get too smug. I've got all the railroads." Leslie glanced at her watch as she finished her soda. "Got to run, Kel," she said, throwing the empty cup in the trash basket.

"Wait," Kelley said.

Leslie turned.

"You know that skin graft Monday? The one on my face?"

"What about it, Kelley?"

"I guess I don't understand. I mean, if they take more skin off my leg, behind my thigh, to put on my face, then . . . well, what happens to my leg?"

Leslie put her hands on her hips. "They didn't explain that to you?"

"Yeah, but I didn't understand it all."

"Kelley, you should never be afraid to ask questions. You have a right to know what's happening to your own body. *Always.*"

She came back to stand closer to Kelley. "What they're going to do is take another layer of skin, a board they call it, from the back of your leg. From a different place, of course. And they're going to graft it on the burned portions of your face: your forehead, your cheek, up toward your ear. It's basically the same operation you had for your hand, Kelley."

"So the back of my leg will hurt again?"

Leslie nodded. "It'll hurt. Just like the other graft. Remember, taking that layer off leaves you with the equivalent of another second-degree burn."

"Ouch."

Leslie pressed her lips together in sympathy. "Kelley, you've been through worse already."

Kelley straightened the crumpled napkin in her hand and nervously tore small notches in its edge. "Will this leave scars on my leg?"

"Yes," Leslie said. "It will leave scars."

Kelley swallowed. Then, in the summer, when she wore a bathing suit, she'd have these big red patches on her legs. Her eye began to water.

"Next time they'll take the donor skin from somewhere else," Leslie said.

"I know," Kelley said soberly. "My butt."

Leslie raised her eyebrows. "Well, at least it won't be very noticeable. Unless you wear a *thong*—or go to one of those nude beaches in France."

Kelley couldn't imagine. She tried to smile but couldn't.

"Is there anything else?" Leslie asked.

Kelley hesitated. "I'm just scared," she said.

Leslie took Kelley's left hand. "Don't be afraid," she said. "Dr. Brewer and Dr. LaMotte won't let anything happen to you. You know that."

As she spoke, Leslie's identification badge swung forward from a long silver chain around her neck. Kelley didn't think the picture looked much like Leslie, even though she could tell it was her. The short dark hair, the straight bangs, the dark glasses. They were Leslie from another era. Her hair was longer now, streaked with gray and pulled back with a clip at the nape of her neck. Leslie Anne Jakowski, R.N. It pleased Kelley that they both shared Anne for a middle name. It made the connection between them a little stronger, a little more special.

"I mean it. You'll be fine," Leslie assured her. "I'm on duty all day Monday. I'll be here. So don't worry, okay?"

"I'll try," Kelley said. She knew Leslie had to go. She was a busy nurse, with lots of other patients.

Leslie handed her the earphones to her portable CD player. "Here, why don't you listen to something and rest this afternoon before they bring dinner?"

Kelley nodded bravely, and Leslie left, closing the door softly behind her.

She looked at the earphones in her hand. They were greasy with the white cream they smeared on her face beneath the dressings. Every time she listened to music, the earphones got messy. Not wanting to deal with it, she set them down and picked up the dice to the Monopoly game.

Secretly, Kelley had always been superstitious. She lifted her feet whenever they crossed railroad tracks in the car. She held her breath going by a cemetery. She never walked under a ladder. And she always ate the black-eyed peas her mother made on New Year's Day. So she rolled the dice just one more time—to see—and when double fours came up, she clutched the two white cubes in her left hand and held them tight. They were still in her grip when the banging of the metal tray cart outside her door woke her for dinner at four-thirty.

# four

THE TELEPHONE RANG, STARTLING KELLEY. It was Leah, calling from Paris. The sound of her sister's voice, coming from across an entire ocean, was like a dream.

"Kelley! Are you there?"

"Leah," Kelley said sleepily.

"Hi! How are you? I haven't talked to you for almost a week."

"You haven't?" Kelley had little concept of time. Days and weeks still ran together.

"No. The last time we talked, you were really out of it. Remember? I called right after you had that skin graft operation on your face?"

"Oh," Kelley said, truly not remembering.

"Mom says the graft took right away. What do you think? Has it made a difference?"

"A difference?"

"Yeah. The graft."

Kelley didn't respond.

"Kel, you there?"

"Yes."

"Did the graft help? I mean, you've looked at it, haven't you?"

"No. No, I haven't," Kelley said slowly, and there was another pause, with Leah perhaps wondering why Kelley hadn't looked—it was an innocent enough question—and Kelley not wanting to offer up the fact that she hadn't seen her face at all since the accident.

"It's wrapped up," Kelley said.

"Oh . . . of course it is. Well, does it hurt?"

"Not much," Kelley said. "Actually, my leg hurts more."

"Your leg?"

"My broken leg."

"Gosh, Kelley. I forgot about the leg." Leah's voice faded, and there was an audible sigh.

Kelley didn't want her to be sad. "Tell me what you're doing," Kelley said. Leah's life was like a storybook to her. She loved hearing the details of it.

"Nothing I'm doing is very important. Not compared to—"

"Leah, *please,*" Kelley implored.

"Okay," Leah said reluctantly. "I'm studying, of course. I have one more exam and I'm finished. Then I'll probably go jogging. I'm trying to do five miles a day. Plus I have my dance class, you know. But I figure that'll sweat off a few more calories, so that's good. I'm eating like a pig over here. Anyway, let's see. Tomorrow night, we're all invited, the American students, to a special dinner at the home of a university professor."

"Cool," Kelley said.

"Oh, Kelley, this is so much fun, I can't tell you. You absolutely have to do a year abroad when you're in college."

"Oh, I will," Kelley assured her.

"It's the best thing I've ever done. And it's so clear to me now what I want to do."

"What?" Kelley asked.

"Dance and teach French. I'm even thinking I'd love to live in Paris."

"All the time?"

"Maybe."

"Did you tell Mom?"

"Not really. Not yet. It's just a thought."

Just a thought. But it was unsettling to Kelley to think that her sister might choose to live in another country. Lucky Leah. She had always known who she was and what she wanted to do.

Kelley had no idea what she wanted to do in life. If she had a talent, she sure hadn't discovered it yet. She was just an average kid. She had to have a tutor in math just to get C's. And as far as looks went—well, you could probably forget that now. It used to be she was okay, even if she did have pale skin sprinkled with freckles. In the summer, when her friends got so tanned and healthy-looking, Kelley had to smear on tons of sunblock so she wouldn't end up looking like an overripe tomato. But she had thick brown hair that took on gold highlights in the sun, and even Leah said Kelley had a "cute figure."

Still, not a single thing about Kelley made her stand out, the way Alison's beautiful long hair made people comment, or the way Leah's laugh lingered like a musical note long after she'd left the room.

"Kelley, are you still there?" Leah sounded concerned.

"I'm sorry."

"Well, have you?"

"Have I what?"

"Have you heard from Dad?"

"I think so—a postcard," Kelley said, vaguely recalling the picture of a gray bank of buildings. "From Tulsa or Kansas City, somewhere like that. I think he was at a computer conference."

The conversation ended soon afterward, but something from it continued to gnaw at Kelley. Leah wanting to stay in Paris? No, something deeper. If she wanted to, she could have traced it back.

Kelley glanced at the clock. Still four or five hours before her mother would arrive.

Filling time. Killing time.

Sometimes, in the hospital, there were stretches when time seemed to stand still, when not even television or music or a new magazine could wear away another five minutes. Times when Kelley could actually *feel* her one uncovered eye glaze over as she watched the long second hand on the clock above the television set making its end-less, lugubrious circle. Times when Kelley felt as though she was treading air the way you tread water, her eye fastened to the clock as the sounds of the hospital droned on around her: the muffled voices, the doors closing, the metal trays being set down, the cart with the squeaking wheel rolling *clunkety clunkety* down the tiled hallway, the telephone ringing in someone else's room, Leonard crying as he struggled to eat.

If she was lucky her mind would hook onto something and drift.

Sometimes, she thought about school. The clock said 2:10 P.M. It was Wednesday. If she were in school she would be leaving science and shuffling, two doors down, to literature class. She could see Mrs. Scherpa wearing one of her flashy silk scarves. She knew how to tie them so many ways.

The accident was on a Wednesday. What were they reading that day? Jamie had sat across from her in the circle with a hair scrunchie on her wrist, constantly pulling her hair into a ponytail, fixing it, letting it down, playing with it again.

The book had *mountain* in the title. *The Mountain? My Side of the Mountain* by Jean Craighead George. They had just finished reading it. It was about a boy living in the wilderness. He gathered nuts and berries and slept in the trunk of a tree. He killed a deer and tanned its hide.

That day in class, the day of the accident, they talked about conflict.

*Like a story, a novel has conflict . . .*

Mrs. Scherpa pressed so hard on the blackboard that sometimes pieces of chalk broke off. The end of her scarf, draped over one shoulder, fluttered as though it had a life of its own. She turned to be sure everyone was copying this down.

*A character may challenge circumstances that cannot be changed . . .*

The literature book had perished in the fire, but Kelley could still see its bright green cover, the words *Discovering Literature* in white with gold trim. The book was in her backpack, in the backseat. Kelley had thrown it there when she and her mother got in the car to drive home.

They were out of breath because they had run to the car. Across the parking lot at the mall. Night was closing in. Lights coming on as people hurried to get home. Though it was late April, the temperature had dropped suddenly, and a cold wind blew trash by their feet. Kelley had quickly settled herself in the front seat of her mother's car and pulled her sweater on. She rubbed her arms to get warm and then rooted in her lunch bag to find the apple she hadn't eaten at lunch.

"You're still hungry? After all that food?" Her mother was shivering, too, as she started the car and turned on the heat.

"Well, not hungry exactly. But I did want dessert."

"I'm sorry, Kel. If I didn't have these people coming."

Kelley had groaned. All day, she had managed *not* to think about selling their house. Then, midway through dinner—they had eaten at the Macaroni Grill—her mother had suddenly remembered that someone was coming to see it.

"I still wish we didn't have to do this," Kelley had grumbled.

"What? Sell the house?" Her mother sighed as she backed up the car. "Gosh, Kelley. You know I don't want to—and maybe we won't! I don't know. But it's a struggle for me. When your father and I bought that house we had two full incomes, and waterfront taxes weren't anything like they are today. It costs a lot to keep that place up on my own. I just can't do it. Especially with Leah in college."

"So there's still a chance we won't?"

Her mother had smiled tiredly. "Still a chance," she said, before picking up the car phone to make a call as she maneuvered her way out of the parking lot.

Kelley squeezed her eyes shut and pulled up the sheet in her hospital bed. She did not want to recall any more than that. She knew that twenty minutes later she had been pulled through the window of a burning car.

She couldn't help herself, though.

Sometimes, Kelley even thought about the truck driver who did this to her. His name was Quentin Hall. He was twenty-two years old, only two years older than Leah, and came from Virginia, a town called Burgess. He was hauling lumber the night of the accident. Some of it spilled on the road. He broke his collarbone and injured his eyes in the collision. That's all Kelley knew. It's all she wanted to know, really. She never asked about him.

Quentin Hall. It was a stupid name, she thought. Like two last names or the name of a building at a college. People wondered if he had been drinking. They made him take a test for it, the night of the accident, but the lawyer Kelley's mother hired said the test showed Quentin Hall was sober.

In weak moments, when her mother was late, or when Leslie didn't come because she had the day off—or on stormy days such as this one, when rain streaked down her wide windows like endless tears, Kelley thought about Quentin Hall. He was a name without a face. A bad character in a bad story, except that he was alive somewhere—laughing, Kelley imagined. Maybe planning a picnic for Memorial Day weekend like everyone else in the hospital, while Kelley had to stay in her bed day after day, getting sponge baths and using a horrible, humiliating bedpan because she still couldn't get up to shower or go to the bathroom.

And now, on top of surgery and painful dressings and torturous hand exercises, Kelley had to push those wretched tongue depressors between her teeth—one by one—in order to stretch the new skin and mending muscles near her mouth. She was up to four tongue depressors, stacked one upon the other. It hurt. But Quentin Hall didn't know that. She wondered if he ever once thought about her. Was he ever sad? Did he pray for her?

Why didn't he apologize? When she thought about him, her teeth clenched and her stomach grew tight. Kelley had never hated anyone in her life. But it was possible that she hated Quentin Hall. If she could, she thought, she'd force him to eat a whole box full of tongue depressors!

"Kelley, how are you feeling?"

Dr. LaMotte's voice made her jump.

"I didn't mean to scare you."

"It's okay," she said, trying to sit up a little.

A nurse accompanied Dr. LaMotte and, together, they proceeded to remove the gauze that covered the right half of Kelley's face.

When they finished, the surgeon lifted Kelley's chin gently and studied her face closely. What did he see? she wondered. He had promised Kelley he was going to "fix her up." So had he?

Dr. LaMotte patted her hand. "It looks good. Real good. Remember, though, Kelley, there are going to be some things we can't do for another few months. Some things we can't do for another year."

What things? Why a year? Kelley wanted to know but was afraid to ask.

Instead, she inquired timidly, "When can I go home?"

Dr. LaMotte smiled. "Hopefully in a couple of weeks. When it's time for more surgery, you'll come back."

Kelley swallowed hard. "I understand," she said.

Just then, her mother strode briskly into the room with her canvas bag. Dr. LaMotte pulled off his plastic gloves and shook hands with her. "We're quite pleased,

Mrs. Brennan. The graft took beautifully. There's a place near the corner of her mouth we need to watch, but the rest of it looks great."

The doctor gave Kelley a thumbs-up and smiled at her. "We'll talk some more later, okay?"

When he left the room, so did Kelley's mom. She knew they talked about her in the hallway or out of sight in someone's office. She didn't much like it, but there was nothing she could do. She didn't even ask what they said because she knew there were things they wouldn't tell her.

But then again, there was safety in not knowing. She could never say this out loud, but to Kelley, if you didn't know how bad it really was, then you could still hope for the best.

# five

"LOOK WHAT I FOUND IN the hallway," Kelley's mother announced as she returned to the room. She beckoned with her hand, and, slowly, Liesel and Alison appeared from behind her.

Kelley's heart leaped at the sight of her two best friends. They looked at each other, no one knowing what to say, until Liesel stepped forward and broke the silence.

"Kel, you look so much better," she said. "It must be a relief to have all those bandages off your face." She smiled brightly, but Kelley could see the corners of her mouth quiver. What did she see? Was it that bad? Kelley wished now that she had found the courage to look at herself first, before her friends saw her.

Kelley's eyes flicked to Alison. It was her first visit. Did that explain why she hung back a little?

"Yeah, you . . . you look great, Kelley," Alison faltered.

Kelley knew they were just saying that, but she understood. She didn't hold it against them.

Behind her friends, in the doorway, Liesel's mother stretched her neck to see and blew Kelley a kiss. "Are you feeling better?" she asked.

Kelley shrugged. "A little," she said.

Alison came closer. Pretty Alison with her long dark hair and porcelain skin. She had on new earrings, big silver hoops that seemed as large as her sad dark eyes. "We miss you," she said.

"Big time," Liesel added. She had a cold sore on her lip. Poor Liesel. She either ate too much or got a cold sore whenever she was "stressed out."

"I miss you guys, too," Kelley told them.

"So you need to hurry up and get out of here," Liesel urged.

Alison nodded. "It's not the same without you," she said, her voice shaking.

Kelley dropped her eyes. She hoped that Alison wasn't going to start crying.

Liesel's mother moved forward and put her arms around the two girls. "Hey! Why don't you show Kelley what you brought?"

Eagerly, the girls rushed to a bag on the floor and began unwrapping things in tissue paper. Kelley watched, amused, as they pulled out china teacups and saucers, silver spoons, and a plate full of decorated sugar cookies and brownies.

While the mothers went for hot water, the girls set up

the tea party on Kelley's tray and then launched into a frenzy of interior decorating, festooning the room with colorful paper chains, silver balloons, and dozens of silk flowers.

"You guys. I don't believe this," Kelley said, shaking her head. Someday, she would tell them how much it meant to her.

Alison and Liesel exchanged smiles and sat down to drink the tea that the mothers had prepared before leaving again, so the girls could be alone.

"Well, you haven't missed much at school." Alison pulled up a chair by Kelley's bed.

"No," Liesel agreed, sitting beside Alison and selecting a cookie from the plate on Kelley's tray. "It's been really boring."

"I can't believe all the work I'll have to make up," Kelley said.

"Oh, but we'll help," Liesel assured her. "Don't worry about that. I can definitely help you with the math."

"And you know Mrs. Scherpa," Alison jumped in to say. "She's so nice, she probably won't make you do anything. She didn't that week I was out with strep throat."

There was a pause. Liesel popped an entire cookie into her mouth and checked the elastic that held back her thick, frizzy red hair. Alison fidgeted with the choker around her neck, then stirred her tea again. "Oh!" she suddenly remembered. "We beat St. Mary's in lacrosse!"

Liesel's face lit up. "Seven to six!" she burst out, covering her mouth because it was full.

"It was a *great* game," Alison exclaimed. "Daniel scored five of the goals!"

Kelley looked down at her tea.

"He said to say 'hi,' " Alison added.

Kelley lifted the teacup to her mouth.

While they were all sipping their tea, Kelley's physical therapist came into the room.

"Well, hell-o," Anita greeted the girls. "Sorry to intrude during visiting hours, Kelley, but we need to do one quick thing before I leave for the day."

Kelley didn't want her friends to go. "Can they stay?" she asked.

"Sure. That's okay," Anita replied.

Alison and Liesel stepped back to make way for Anita. At the same time, the mothers returned. Together, they all watched as Anita removed the splint from Kelley's right hand.

"This won't take long," the therapist promised. "Would you like to show your friends what you can do first?"

Kelley straightened her right hand and slowly folded all five fingers in to make a small fist.

"Kelley, *yes!* That's wonderful!" her mother cheered.

Kelley glanced up at her friends, both of whom were smiling.

"Remember when you thought that was impossible?" Anita asked.

Kelley nodded. She had to admit she had despaired more than once.

"You've come a long way," Anita reminded her. "But

now, as the skin heals, we need to keep pressure on it so the scar doesn't get all puffy. I've got something I want you to wear." She placed a brown glove on the bed in front of Kelley. It was meshlike, with a zipper up the back and no fingertips.

"It's a pressure garment made by a company called Jobst, so we all call it a Jobst," Anita told her. "This is a Jobst for your hand."

Kelley was confused. "A glove? A what kind of garment?"

"Let me explain. If you just let the scar tissue grow back the way it wanted, it would grow back all puffed up. It's called hypertrophic scarring." Anita made a face. "Ugly. Trust me, you do *not* want it to happen. We need to put constant pressure on the new skin to keep it smooth. People who have bad burns on their arms and legs wear Jobst garments, like tight long johns, made out of the same elastic material.

"Here. Try it on." She held the glove open while Kelley eased her hand in, wincing when the fabric brushed the tender new skin growing on her knuckles. When it covered her hand, Anita gently closed the little zipper so the glove was snug. Kelley tried to open and close her fist now and couldn't believe how hard it was to make this simple motion.

"You'll get used to it," Anita assured her. "In another day or two you won't feel the tightness at all."

"Remember when you had to wear that retainer in your mouth?" Kelley's mother asked. "After a while you didn't even know it was there."

Sure, Kelley remembered. But she was not convinced that this glove was going to be as easy.

"The important thing is that you have to wear the Jobst all the time. Twenty-three hours a day," Anita emphasized.

"Twenty-three?" Kelley looked up at her.

"You have an hour off to bathe or take a shower without it."

"A shower?"

Anita tilted her head. "Yes, someday you'll be taking showers again. Just as soon as you get those pins out of your leg."

Kelley almost laughed. Good news always came with some bad news around here. She would finally be able to get up and take a shower, but she would have to wear that dumb glove now.

"Okay. One more item on the agenda and I will skedaddle." Anita stood with her hands on her hips. "Do you like to draw?"

Alison and Liesel had been quiet, but now Liesel piped up. "Tell her, Kel—about the mural."

"The mural?" Anita asked.

Kelley blushed. "I helped do this Maryland mural at school, but everyone worked on it."

"Kelley, come *on!*" Alison protested. "You designed it—and you drew most of it!" She turned to Anita. "This mural is so awesome you wouldn't believe it."

"It's a scene," Liesel added, "with crabs and seagulls—and a sailboat."

"A skipjack," Kelley gently corrected her.

"A skipjack, whatever. It covers an entire wall in the lobby at school."

"Not only that," Alison continued. "But Kelley is the best doodler in our class. She has drawn a million ladybugs for me."

"And *pigs!*" Liesel hastened to add.

Anita raised her eyebrows at Kelley.

"Well, Alison loves ladybugs, and Liesel loves pigs," Kelley explained.

"This is good!" Anita said, nodding and chuckling. She put a small board in front of Kelley and gave her some paper and pencils. "I want you to start drawing, okay? Pigs, ladybugs—anything. Just keep that right hand moving."

The visit from her friends had cheered her up. Only after everyone left did Kelley try to draw. She was glad she had waited because it was difficult to even hold the pencil. When she finally managed an awkward grip, she could barely write her name or make a circle. She remembered a game she used to play with her mother. Her mother would scribble on a piece of paper and then hand the paper to Kelley, who would transform the nonsense into a picture—a mouse nibbling cheese, a bunny wearing eyeglasses. It never ceased to amaze her mother, and it made Kelley proud.

For a moment, the pencil went limp in her hand as Kelley stared at the paper in front of her, recalling that smiling little girl, remembering home. She thought of the blue heron, squawking at the crack of dawn and of the many times she had tried to sneak up on him, sometimes hiding behind bushes as she inched her way down to the water. There was a path to the water. In spring, daffodils grew in bunches along the path. She began to sketch them, recalling how the flowers smelled like fresh rainwater when their fat, moist stems were snapped.

In the days that followed, Kelley took up the pencil and struggled to sketch other memories from home: her precious pony, dozing in the midday sun with a white egret perched on his back; Tigger, curled up asleep on the striped window seat; Leah in a long dress, her hair tied back with a big bow, the way she wore it as Clara in *The Nutcracker* ballet. Everything was done in black and white, with lots of shadowing.

Leslie, Anita, and the other nurses on duty made a fuss over the pictures. Her mother, too. She bought a big blue scrapbook and a glue stick and helped Kelley preserve each drawing on its own page.

"You should take art lessons," Liesel urged one day when she was visiting. "I'm *not* kidding!"

But Kelley knew they were just saying these things to cheer her up. The pictures were rudimentary and unpolished, drawn in the short periods of time between pain. Drawn to exercise her hand in the tight brown glove.

And did anyone notice? None of the people she drew had faces.

# six

"IT'S TIME," LESLIE SAID.

She stood by the edge of Kelley's bed, holding a mirror with a short handle. She didn't say anything more. She didn't have to.

Kelley knew instantly what Leslie was going to do. And she decided, then and there, that there were some things you had to do yourself, especially in the hospital, where everything, it seemed, was done *to* you or *for* you, and you had nothing to say about it.

"I know it's time," Kelley replied. "And I know I have to. But I want to wait. Just a little more. Please?"

Leslie raised her eyebrows. "It's been more than three weeks, Kelley. You're going to have to look at your face sooner or later. It might as well be now."

"One more day. Tomorrow. I *promise*."

Leslie locked eyes with her.

"I swear to God," Kelley said, holding up her gloved hand as though taking an oath. "Tomorrow we'll look."

Leslie seemed uncertain. She set the hand mirror down, and as soon as she did her name was called on the intercom. There was an emergency. "I'll be back," she promised, before rushing out.

While she was away, Kelley slid the mirror into the drawer beneath her bed tray.

Soon afterward, Kelley's mother came in carrying a big envelope stuffed with cards and letters from Kelley's school. Even first and second graders from the lower school had drawn pictures for her: flowers, birds, lots of rainbows, and messages saying, "Get Well Soon." As though she only had a bad case of the flu, Kelley thought. None of this stuff made any difference. She was not only the class project, but the school project as well, and she didn't like it.

Kelley squeezed the ball of pink therapy putty in her right hand as hard as she could and kneaded it, over and over, to exercise her hand and fingers. The putty, like soft clay, was kept in a plastic bag so it wouldn't get her glove greasy.

Glancing up, she could see her mother was disappointed.

"One more thing—a photograph," her mother said hopefully, pulling out a large, eight-by-ten-inch print. She handed it to Kelley.

"It's from Daniel."

Kelley set the putty down and took the picture into her hands. The photograph was strange. She began to worry it was some kind of a weird joke. A parking lot with seagulls and gravel? And suddenly it hit her!

It was the roof of the Islander Hardware Store. Not seagulls, but little least terns. Squinting, Kelley pulled the photograph close. Little gray birds with black caps sitting protectively on their eggs. In the background was the fence, the chicken wire they had installed at the edge of the roof so the baby birds wouldn't fall off once they were big enough to walk but still couldn't fly. They had done it on a cloudy day. It had started to drizzle that day, but they kept on working, anyway. Afterward, they had gone back to Kelley's house to make tacos and listen to music.

Kelley had been planning to go back up on the roof in late May to count the eggs before they hatched. She was going to make a log. Give each egg and nest a number in case they had to be moved.

She wondered if someone else would be taking her place now.

Now that she couldn't be there.

Now that things were different.

She could feel the expression fade from her face.

Her face.

"It's the project—"

"I know," Kelley cut her mother off. "I know what it is." It was just that she wouldn't be part of this project now. Another chunk of her life sliced off and gone forever.

"Daniel thought you'd like to see how it's going," her mother said gently. "He went up there special."

Kelley placed the picture on the pile of second-grade drawings.

"You don't like it?"

"It's nice," Kelley said. But inside she didn't care about the terns anymore. She had no feeling for them. If they fell off the roof, so what? Life could be cruel.

"Tell him thanks," she said, picking up the therapy putty again.

Her mother thumbtacked the picture to the bulletin board. Then she tried to get Kelley interested in something, a game of cards or checkers, but Kelley wasn't in the mood. At one point, she even handed Kelley a piece of paper with a scribble on it. Kelley looked at it silently for a moment. She knew it was the old game. Her mother wanted her to turn the scribble into a picture. "I just don't feel like it right now," Kelley mumbled, handing back the paper.

Her mother didn't skip a beat. "Well, I hear you helped with your own dressings today."

"Yeah, it was a lot of fun," Kelley deadpanned.

"Grandma Brennan called from Florida last night. She wondered if you'd like to have some nice fresh oranges shipped up."

"Sure."

For a few more minutes her mother remained, tidying up the room, rereading the Get Well cards already tacked to the bulletin board. When visiting hours were up, she tucked Kelley's stuffed panda into her arms and blew a final kiss before disappearing around the door.

Kelley held her panda and waited until she was sure she was alone. She waited until after the evening snack was delivered and night medication was dispensed. Finally, when the hallways were quiet and the doors closed, she put the panda down, flicked on the light by her bed, and swallowed hard.

She took the mirror out and lifted it, slowly, cautiously. But nothing could have prepared her. Not really. Because what she saw in the mirror was the cold, hard face of a stranger.

Two ears were there, one of them a little red and scabby. There was a set of lips, some teeth, a familiar nose. But an eyebrow was missing and one entire side of this stranger's face was a different color. A dark, pinkish brown. Leslie had warned her new skin would look that way until there was good blood circulation.

And there were tiny little scabs all over. Almost like acne, Kelley thought, except she knew it wasn't. Those would be the tiny pricks they made in the sheet of skin they had grafted onto her face. Little holes. For drainage, they said.

She took a breath. The whole right side of her face had a shine to it from the ointment, the bacitracin they smeared on because of the graft. In fact, she could still see a couple of bloody spots that hadn't healed, near the corner of her mouth and under her eye.

The eye. Was it really her eye? That moist little slit surrounded by puffy, discolored flesh?

She made contact with the dark circle struggling to see out, and she knew she was staring into her own soul. Yet, even then she didn't scream or cry out because inside she felt as cold and empty as a cardboard box, as though her heart had been lifted out, leaving a wide, dry hole in her chest.

Shock. Maybe that's what shock did, Kelley thought. It made you feel detached somehow. Kelley didn't understand why she didn't freak out and scream. She simply stared back at the stranger in the mirror. And she thought of the state of New York.

The burn on the right side of her face had left a red scar shaped like the state of New York. Kelley knew this shape from the wooden jigsaw puzzle she and Leah had as little kids. New York was easy. Not as easy as Texas or California. But it was big, and it fit around one of the Great Lakes painted on the board. Lake Ontario, she guessed. Lake Ontario was right where her eye was.

She was lucky, they all said, because she didn't lose that eye.

Or break her back.

Hey! Or crush her leg so badly she would never walk on it again!

She was lucky, they all said, because she was thrown *under* the dashboard instead of *through* the windshield into this speeding truck that had come from out of nowhere.

She was lucky, they all said, because even though she was burned when the engine caught fire, she was pulled out *mere seconds* before the entire car burst into flames.

No. "Not lucky enough," she whispered out loud. She knew this for a fact during the moment when she first saw her face and felt that cold shock and then the wall of hot tears slowly building behind her eyes, spilling out onto one cheek that had no feeling because the nerve endings were gone.

There were times, and this was one of them, when Kelley wished she *had* gone through the windshield, that a pair of hands had *not* come through the window in time or that the flames had *consumed* her instead of merely searing one side of her body like a piece of meat on the grill!

Her mother, her friends, her teachers—no one could begin to understand the loss she suffered, the horror and fear of being disfigured for life, the pain!

"You know what they have to do, don't you?" Kelley had asked Alison just yesterday. Alison had a gift on her lap, her jacket still on. "Every day, they pull my skin off."

Alison put a hand to her mouth. Tears welled in her eyes.

It was only the second time Alison had come to visit Kelley on the burn unit, and Kelley could tell that her friend was still intimidated by the environment. The medicine smell, the moaning in the room next door, the occasional swish-swish urgency of a nurse bounding down the hall. It took a while before you really got used to it.

"Really, Alison. Twice a day they come in and pull the dead skin off my leg with tweezers and Q-tips. They used to do it to my hand, too. And my face. It's called debridement. They only do it twenty minutes at a time because they know you can't stand it. And they come in and give you pain medication before they do it. They teach you hypnosis, too. You know. *Imagine you're back at the barn, Kelley, saddling up EO for a ride. It's a gorgeous day. Bright sun, blue sky. You can smell the hay and feel the smooth, worn saddle leather . . .* But it never blocks it out completely. How can it? And you know what it feels like?"

Alison's wide eyes begged her to stop.

"It feels like they're pulling your skin off!"

Alison ran out of the room. Kelley knew she wouldn't come back.

Leslie had warned Kelley some of her friends wouldn't be able to handle it.

But Kelley knew she had been mean to Alison. She had *driven* her away.

"I wish I was dead. Dead and buried in the ground," she told her mother the next day.

"Kelley, stop! Don't say that!" Her mother dropped the canvas bag and rushed to Kelley's bedside.

But Kelley couldn't wait to say it. She had waited a whole twelve hours to say it.

"I don't want to be alive! I don't! I don't want to live if I have to look like this!"

Her mother glanced at the mirror on the bed tray.

"No, no, no, Kelley! You have to be strong. They're working on it. They're not done yet."

"It doesn't matter! It's never going to look the same! You *know* it's not!"

"But it's going to be all right."

"It's not! You're a liar!"

"Kelley, please—"

"How can I go back to school looking like this? The kids'll be freaked!"

"They won't!"

"They *will!* I can't even face my friends!"

Her mother's voice was tense but calm. "Kelley, you have already faced your friends. And they did *not* turn away."

"Get out of here!" Kelley hollered.

"Don't be angry—!" her mother begged.

"I have a right to be angry!" Kelley yelled.

Her mother touched her hand. She was shaking; there were tears in her eyes, too.

But the rush of anger had been spent; Kelley looked at her. "I just want to die, Mommy. I just want to die."

"Oh, Kelley, please don't say that. I can't live without you."

Even her mother's arms around her didn't make it better.

"Oh, God," Kelley cried softly into the brown glove covering her face. "Why did this happen to me? Why?"

# seven

THEY BROUGHT IN A DOLL the day they told Kelley about the mask.

The doll's name was Beth. She was a big doll, about twenty-four inches tall, with chunks of her short-cropped blond hair missing, exposing her pink plastic scalp. One eye sort of wavered, half shut, making her look kind of sleepy—or drunk. Still, Beth appeared lovable with her one wide blue eye and her little red rosebud mouth. Kelley considered herself way beyond the doll stage, but even *she* had the urge to reach out and hug Beth to her.

"Now. Kelley. Do you remember when we talked about how scar tissue grows back puffy?" Anita asked. Leslie stood beside her.

Kelley, meanwhile, had turned her attention to Anita's

diamond ring. It was an engagement ring. She had told Kelley that her fiancé's name was Tyrone Jamal, but she called him T.J. He was a student at the police academy, an expert in tae kwan do. He could kick a cinder block in half with his heel.

"Do you remember when we talked about that? The day you got your Jobst glove?" Anita persisted.

Kelley nodded. She was fascinated by the diamond's glittering facets. She wondered how much T.J. had paid for it.

"Kelley."

Reluctantly, she focused on Anita, and Beth, who was wearing a miniature set of Jobst stockings and a long-sleeved Jobst jersey the color of wet sand. She was even wearing tiny matching gloves like the one on Kelley's right hand.

But Kelley already knew about the Jobst garments. She didn't need a doll to understand it.

Anita was waiting. "Kelley, please. Do you remember?"

Kelley's eyes flashed at her. "Yes, I remember! Hypersonic—hypertrophic scarring! I'm not stupid, you know!"

Kelley dropped her head. She hadn't meant to be insulting. *You're losing control again,* she warned herself deep inside.

"I guess I'm not myself today," she apologized. "I can't imagine why."

She looked back up to see if Anita would forgive her and saw that the doll had been stood up right in front of her, on the edge of the bed.

Only this time, Kelley noticed that Beth also had some sort of a *thing* strapped on her head. A kind of clear plastic shield over her face, with holes cut in it for eyes, nose, and mouth. Like a see-through Halloween mask. Weird, Kelley thought—until the horror of it began to sink in.

"The mask will do the same for your face, Kelley—"

"Oh, wait a minute—" she started. She could feel the blood drain from her face and the invisible belt of panic tighten around her chest. She should have known something was up when Anita came to her room with Leslie and they closed the door. They had this planned!

"I'm not wearing that—"

"You had a third-degree burn on your right cheek, extending up around your eye and back to your ear—"

Kelley was shaking her head. "No!"

Leslie came and put an arm around her shoulders. "Kelley," she said into her ear. "This is part of recovery."

Kelley tried to push her away. "No way!"

"Let me finish," Anita said firmly, placing one of her hands on Kelley's arm and looking her hard in the eye.

"All the grafting, all the skin growing back in is just like the skin on your hand. It's been two weeks since your face graft, Kelley. It'll come back in all puffed up and hard unless you restrain it."

"But I'll look like a freak!"

"If you want your skin to grow back smooth—"

"No! Don't make me wear that!"

"Kelley, you'll be more of a freak if you *don't* wear it!"

Kelley turned her head away. She knew it was useless to argue. They were only doing their job. She stared at the wall of her room and couldn't help the silent tears that came.

"How long?" she asked wearily, turning back to Anita.

Anita's sad eyes warned her. "A long time, Kelley."

"A long time," she repeated, her voice wavering. "Like what? A couple weeks? A month?"

Anita put her other hand on Kelley's knee and gripped it. "At least a year."

Kelley closed her eyes.

A year. Twelve months. Three hundred and sixty-five days. Twenty-four hours a day. No, twenty-three. They would probably give her an hour off a day to take a bath or a shower.

"As much as you don't like it, it's going to help you in the long run," Anita was saying. She had the mask Kelley would wear and a plaster of Paris mold in her hands, shaped like Kelley's head. "The impression was made while you were asleep, during the last skin-graft operation. This enabled them to make a plastic mask that fits your face perfectly, putting pressure on the burn wounds."

She put the mold down. "It is our face, Kelley, more than our voices, or the words we speak, or the emotions we let in, or let out, that presents each one of us to the world."

"Which is why seeing a face is so important," Leslie added. She took Kelley's left hand and, gently, ran her thumb across it. "Anytime there is an abnormality—something different—people react. They're afraid, Kel. Not that you're a monster or anything like that. They're afraid of what they don't understand. A lot of times people simply don't know what to do or what to say."

74

Anita tried to explain. "What you've got to do, Kelley, is direct attention away from the burn, away from the mask, to *you*—to the person within. Let that personality of yours come shining through."

"You have to learn to be good at second impressions, Kel," Leslie added.

Anita smiled hopefully. "They used to make a Jobst stocking for the face, Kelley. But the plastic is so much better because it can put more pressure on the scar where it needs to, to keep that skin from getting puffy."

Leslie lifted the mask up to her own face: "It's better, too, because the plastic is clear and you can see through it."

Kelley sat through this numbly, half listening. But then Anita said something about this wonderful piece of plastic that struck and stuck in Kelley's mind like a spear:

*"So people see a face first,"* she said. *"Then a mask."*

They went on and on, Anita and Leslie, doing their job. *A face first, then a mask.* But while they talked about recovery and rehabilitation, Kelley was already retreating.

When they finished strapping the new pressure mask on her, when the Velcro straps were good and snug, when she saw the world through two small holes, Kelley knew she was truly alone. A prisoner contained in a cell of plastic. She thought of the Phantom of the Opera, unloved, hiding his hideous face behind a mask. Now she would know what it was like.

She would never have to say anything. The mask would say it for her: *I'm a victim. I'm different from you. You'd better leave me alone.*

# eight

THE NEXT DAY KELLEY DIDN'T speak. Not to anyone. Not to Liesel, who called to tell her about the class picnic at Mears Marina. Not to Leslie, who took the plunge and had her hair cut short, up around her ears. Not to her sister, who called from Switzerland. Not even to her mother, who came in off Eastern Avenue at 7:00 P.M. with a picture of Tigger, blown up, in an "I Miss You" heart-shaped frame.

Kelley had made a decision the moment those Velcro tabs were fastened behind her head. If she couldn't be part of life as she knew it, then she would withdraw from it. Maybe—*maybe* in a year or two, when the surgery was done and the mask was gone, she could test the waters of the world once again. Until then, she would hide out.

That way, no one would have to *look* at her and feel *sorry* for her.

Anita and Leslie tried to coax Kelley out of herself. Anita with her boom box and her tapes, guessing at the music Kelley liked because Kelley wouldn't say. And Leslie, sitting there on her break reading *Jacob Have I Loved*, which only made Kelley homesick because it took place on an island in the Chesapeake Bay.

None of it worked.

The child life therapist counseled her.

The pediatric social worker dropped in.

Dr. Brewer. The hospital chaplain. Even a child psychologist pulled up a chair by her bed.

But for now, Kelley had found a silent place deep down where she could crawl inside and bolt the doors. There was a little window to look out, but no one could see in.

One evening, a few days later, Leslie brought in a beautiful meal on a tray adorned with a sprig of pink azalea in a glass bud vase and silverware wrapped in a white linen napkin. There was a steaming plate full of spaghetti with homemade sauce from Kelley's mother, a warm, buttered baguette wrapped in tinfoil, a fresh green salad, and a slice of frosted carrot cake—Kelley's favorite dessert.

"Allow me," Leslie said, lifting a can of Sprite and pouring it into a wineglass full of chopped ice. She set it back down on the tray and, with a little flourish of her hands, undid the napkin, shook it out, and handed it to Kelley. "If there's anything else you need, mademoiselle, just ring," she said with a graceful bow.

Only after she left did Kelley notice that on the tray there was also a letter from her aunt Katherine and a copy of the latest *Seventeen* magazine, rolled up and tied with a white ribbon. It was lovely. All of it. Kelley was touched by their efforts. If she was speaking, she would have thanked them.

She opened the letter from Aunt Katherine first, but could barely get through the first two lines: *My dearest Kelley, I was in church Sunday and Reverend Grayson was talking about God's plan for us, how everything happens for a reason . . .* Rolling her eyes, Kelley stuffed the unread letter back in its envelope and pushed it under her plate.

She took a deep breath and tried not to let that ruin the beautiful meal. Kelley loved spaghetti. She broke off a piece of the bread, and while she ate, she undid the ribbon on the magazine. It didn't take long. The advertisements more than anything else. *Will bleaching your facial hair leave blotches on your skin? Clearasil: Soft on Skin. Tough on Zits . . .* And on every page, those pretty, flawless faces that would never have to worry about a second impression. Her eyes filled with tears. She pushed the tray away.

But wasn't she like that once? Kelley answered her own question by nodding yes. Everything she wore had to match or be cool: pants with the right amount of bagginess, a shirt with the tank top underneath, the chunky heels, the hair just so. Appearance was *everything*. Didn't

Kelley cry when a pimple showed up on her nose the day the class pictures were being taken? She sucked in her breath at the memory. How incredibly *small*. How meaningless!

Her eyes scanned the next page: *Choosing the right blush. What's your skin tone?* "Burnt Charcoal," Kelley mouthed sarcastically. She could feel the anger building. The last straw came when she glimpsed the beauty columns—a big write-up with pictures—on tweezing eyebrows and how to get the shape right. *Tweezing eyebrows.* She didn't even have two eyebrows like everybody else! By then the magazine had her so ripping mad she flung it, like a Frisbee, toward the door, where it hit and skidded out into the hall, right in front of Dr. Brewer, who was taking some foreign medical students on a tour.

"Not very nice," Leslie scolded her when she came in to take her vitals. "Come on, give me your arm. I need to get your blood pressure."

Kelley pushed up the sleeve of her nightgown.

"These students came all the way from Japan. They're going to think you're nuts, Kelley! They're going to think they're on the psycho ward instead of the burn unit."

Kelley felt her stomach knot up.

Leslie was quiet as she listened for the sounds that measured Kelley's blood pressure. When she finished, she took the stethoscope from her ears, undid the tight sleeve, and continued: "But we all know you're not crazy. Just *angry*. Angry at the world because of what happened. This is the way it is now, Kelley. You have to let that anger go."

She waited a moment, maybe waiting for Kelley to say something, then sighed and left.

Kelley rolled her eyes. But Leslie was right and Kelley knew it. Kelley had known it all along. And now she wanted to get back at someone for what had happened. She knew she was taking it out on the wrong people. After all, it was an accident, and Quentin Hall was the only one to blame.

Wasn't he?


The next day, a bone infection was discovered in Kelley's broken, right leg. Osteomyelitis in the fractured tibia, Dr. Brewer pronounced. Not good. Kelley figured she'd be able to write a medical text if she ever made it out of the hospital. A course of powerful antibiotics was prescribed.

She had already been in the hospital for six weeks, and there had been talk of sending her home soon. She even had new crutches and could walk a short distance. But now, because of the new infection, Kelley would have to stay even longer.

"We're moving you down to pediatrics," Leslie told her, pushing a wheelchair up to her bed.

Kelley frowned.

"Don't worry. We'll be down to take care of you. Same crew. Same nurses. It's just that we need to free up your bed on the burn unit." She tried to coax a smile from Kelley by remaining cheerful. "It's called progress, Kel."

But Kelley didn't respond, and she hated pediatrics.

The entire floor was way too warm, even with the air-conditioning on. Not only that, but every hallway, every room, had that sickly, sweet smell that reminded her of baby-sitting little kids—a nose-wrinkling mélange of cough syrup, stale apple juice, baby powder, and sweaty pajamas.

And talk about dreary, she thought. Her room was hardly more than a closet, and the view out the dirty, grimy window was as dull as the day was long. Nothing green. No rivers or bridges. No traffic reminding her that life was going on. Just an unused parking lot with dead, black, boring asphalt and lifeless, gray, give-me-a-break cement.

The only interesting aspect to these quarters, Kelley discovered, was that if you looked hard to the right outside her window, you could see the big red $X$ with the small white $H$ in it: the concrete helipad where the noisy medevac helicopters landed with new patients. If you were lucky. Lucky? Could that be the right word? Kelley closed her eyes again and had to smile sarcastically, thinking this. In her head, she rephrased it: *If you happened to be looking when the helicopter landed,* you got to see some poor soul strapped to a backboard, neck in a C-collar, already hooked up to bags of this and bags of that, get whisked off to the emergency room.

She watched the first couple of times, then, for some reason, she didn't want to anymore. Only it wasn't that easy *not* to, she discovered. The second day there, first thing in the morning, she heard one of the helicopters coming in and couldn't stop herself. She sat straight up and leaned over, even though it hurt her leg, to watch as the helicopter hovered, then lowered itself, down, down, down, while orderlies in white coats, fighting the wind, rushed out with a stretcher to meet it.

Kelley's heart started thumping because there were parts of this that she remembered now. The rotors whirring—God, they were loud. They sounded *so close*. And the rain falling—hard, stinging pieces of rain. A black night. Silver pain—shooting, piercing stabs—like a thousand needles in one part of her body.

What else? What else? She tried to remember more. But so much had been forgotten. Repressed, some people would say. Blocked out, Kelley knew, by the brick wall she herself had built in her own mind.

But now she wanted to remember. She *needed* to remember. So she began, carefully, to take the bricks down, one by one, and let things come. . . .

Kelley and her mother were in the car. They had left the mall after dinner. Yes, yes. Then what?

Her mother was on the cell phone. Kelley had an apple in her hand. She took a bite from the apple and turned her attention back to a small picture on her lap. It was a color photograph in a plastic frame. Daniel had given it to her after the Earth Day dedication. "Gee, thanks," was all she said. She hoped she hadn't sounded like a jerk.

Absentmindedly, in the car that night, Kelley had pulled on the frog earring. It was dark, but she didn't need any light to see the photograph. Her eyes had already memorized every detail: Eric, Melissa, and Mr. Banker from the Department of Natural Resources, standing in front of a chicken-wire fence, Kelley and Daniel kneeling in front, all of them with goofy smiles and a damp, disheveled look because it had started raining.

All afternoon at school, the day of the accident, Kelley had kept the photograph a secret. She hadn't even shown Liesel or Alison. On the ride home, though, she had wondered what they would say. Alison would be incredibly jealous, of course, but sweet, too, because she was a good friend. Kelley could just hear her: "I hate you! He's the cutest boy in the whole school!"

Suddenly, her mother had asked for something.

"Kelley, reach in my purse and get a token for the bridge, would you?"

Kelley rummaged through her mother's purse for her wallet.

"There aren't any tokens in here," she said.

"Darn. Well, quick then. Get out two fifty."

She folded two bills and put two quarters on top, under her thumb. "Here," she said, carefully handing it to her mother.

Her mother took the money as she slowed the car. When the window was down, she extended her hand toward the attendant. But something had slipped. A quarter fell. A quarter, not a token, had fallen on the ground.

"Geez," her mother griped. When she opened the door, cold air blew in. Her mother retrieved the coin.

"Sorry," she said, handing it over, closing the door, commenting as the car moved forward, "it's starting to rain."

Even through her sweater Kelley felt the sharp chill. She rubbed her arms again to get warm and watched the first heavy drops of rain splat against the windshield.

Suddenly, the rain came harder. In a matter of seconds, a few scattered drops turned into heavy sheets that blocked their view and pounded the metal roof. The windshield wipers thumped double time but could barely keep up. One or two cars ahead of them on the approach to the Chesapeake Bay Bridge slowed and pulled over to the side with their hazard lights blinking. But Kelley's mother kept up her speed behind the 18-wheeler she was following.

"For all I know those people could be sitting in our driveway, waiting for us right now!" her mother exclaimed.

The rain came so hard they could barely see the back of the truck in front of them. Kelley glanced out the side window and saw a guardrail flash by. She knew they were at the pinnacle of the bridge, where the concrete barriers along the road were replaced by a huge, enclosed network of steel. Soon, the road flattened out, and all that height and water was behind them. The tractor-trailer continued straight while Kelley's mother veered off onto the exit to Stevensville. They were five minutes from home. Up ahead, at the end of the exit, a traffic light swayed in the wind, and a green light wavered through a curtain of rain.

Kelley's eyes were on the light. She watched it turn yellow.

And then, she watched the yellow light turn red.

Still, her mother did not slow down.

From the side window, Kelley saw headlights coming toward them. A sharp intake of breath, a hand to her chest—she turned, quickly. "Mom!"

But it was too late.

*Blackness*
*and space.*
*Silver pain,*
*and hard, stinging pieces of rain.*
*Rotors*
*whirring close against her head.*
*And Leslie's voice,*
*reaching,*
*while Kelley watched herself*
*balancing*
*on a narrow path in the night.*

# nine

AT FIRST, KELLEY THOUGHT HER mind was playing tricks on her. Or that maybe she had dreamed about remembering the red light. She *hoped* it was only a dream. But over the next couple of days, it kept showing up in her mind, pushing other things aside. She tried to turn her back on it, tried to slip past it somehow. But that little seed of doubt had taken root and was growing strong.

Sometimes, it frightened Kelley that she could remember the accident. She wondered if that was why she started having so many nightmares. One night she dreamed she hid herself in a closet when the light turned red. In her dream, Kelley pulled the door tight, pressed her face into a cold metal corner, and held her breath. Then, just before the truck hit, she woke up. She could feel her heart racing. Her face was pinched and damp with sweat. Only then did she realize that the new mask was strapped on too tight.

Angrily, she took the mask off and raised her arm to heave it across the room. Then she thought better of the idea and pushed the mask with her feet deep under the covers where no one could find it. It stayed there until the next morning when Anita came looking for her.

"Are you ready for therapy?" she asked.

She brought the wheelchair over to Kelley's bed and put her hands on her hips. "Kelley, where's your mask?"

As she had for a week now, Kelley remained silent.

"Come on, you know better than this."

When Kelley still didn't respond, Anita began running her hands along the bed. She found it, of course, near Kelley's feet.

Kelley didn't fight it. She leaned into Anita's thin shoulder while the therapist put the mask back on.

"You know, sometimes it hurts to get better," Anita told her. She lifted Kelley's chin. "You've got to be strong, Kelley."

Kelley made a weak attempt to sit up.

"Hey. Do you remember Leonard upstairs?"

Of course Kelley remembered Leonard. Leonard crying as he ate his pear. Her sad eyes looked into Anita's, expecting the worst.

"He went home this morning," Anita said brightly. "Nine weeks he was here. And do you know, Kelley, that man amazed me because he never ever gave up. He knew what he had to do to move forward. You do, too, Kelley. You've got to focus on your goal."

Her goal.

What *was* her goal? Kelley wondered.

In her silence, Kelley drew. Abstract shapes. Trees with long, fragile branches that spiraled off the paper or twisted in on themselves. Dark clouds that piled one upon the other. Whirlpools with circles that grew bigger and bigger. Haphazard, dark, crazy stuff. Someone—Kelley couldn't remember who—had said the accident was random. Bad luck. Kelley and her mother were in the wrong place at the wrong time. But it was not totally random, Kelley knew. Not totally.

"Exonerate," her mother said.

Startled, Kelley looked up.

Her mother was out of breath. "The elevator's broken. I had to take the stairs." She held up the Scrabble game. "Do you remember when you put 'exonerate' down on a Triple Word Score and won the game? I thought we could play later."

She set the game down on the bed and placed a fresh ginger ale on the corner of Kelley's tray. Her forehead was moist with sweat and she wore Bermuda shorts, a white T-shirt, her gold choker. Kelley glanced toward the window. It must be hot outside. She hadn't realized.

"Let's see," Mom said, setting her canvas bag on the chair by the foot of Kelley's bed. "I brought you some nice stationery, some art note cards from the Smithsonian catalog, some stamps." She piled them onto the Scrabble game. "And Liesel sent you some CDs. She said to keep them and she'd get them back when you came home."

Like Santa Claus, her mother kept reaching into her bag, hoping, no doubt, the next item would bring joy. "Some little Snickers bars," she said, weighing a bag of Kelley's favorite candy in her hand and raising her eyebrows.

When still Kelley said nothing, *did* nothing, her mother pulled the chair up closer. "Is there anything else I can bring you from home, Kelley?"

Kelley knew this was another invitation to speak. To cut the crap and say something. She glanced up and could see the pain this brought to her mother. The heavy circles under her eyes, the eyes themselves so red and bloodshot and tired. Why were they so bloodshot and tired? Worry? Guilt?

More than anything else in the world Kelley did not want to think that her mother was to blame for the accident. If her mother thought the accident was her fault, she would never forgive herself. Kelley had read about people who suffered from guilt and how it could destroy them. She didn't want that to happen to her mother. She needed her. *Now* more than ever.

But for some reason, she still couldn't open her mouth. Kelley even wondered if she wasn't subconsciously—or maybe consciously—punishing her mother for something that maybe she didn't even do!

"I see you got another postcard from your father," her mother said, looking through some of the mail piled on Kelley's bedside table. "He's been laid off, you know. His company is downsizing." Her mother shook her head. "I don't know what that'll do to his child support."

Her mother shook back her hair and crossed her arms. "I talked to Leah last night," she said. "She called from Vienna. Do you remember how she was going to tour Europe after the second semester? She was supposed to go on to Milan, with that young man she met. He has relatives in Italy. But she's worried about you, Kelley. She says she's coming home."

Their eyes met, and Kelley could see that the pain they shared, the thing they had been through, was now extending to Leah. She would suffer, too. She would give up something she had been planning and looking forward to for a long time. Her mother turned away and picked a piece of lint off her shorts. "I don't know. I told her I wasn't so sure she should do that."

Kelley felt torn.

"What do you think?"

She was stumped. Was this a ploy to make her talk?

Her mother waited.

"Oh, my gosh, Kel!" she suddenly exclaimed. "I completely forgot. I need to make a call. She rummaged in her oversize purse for her cellular telephone. "I'm so sorry, Kelley, but this is really important."

The call went through. "Phyllis, listen, I've got a house that came on the market today," her mother said. "It's got four bedrooms, a huge wraparound porch, an eat-in kitchen with *gorgeous* cherry cabinets and Corian counter-tops, and a big yard for Tommy. Absolutely everything you need. Yes—a fireplace, too."

*Everything you need.* The phrase echoed in Kelley's head. She wondered what it was that *she* absolutely needed. She was sure it was not cherry cabinets and Corian countertops. Not even their house, which her mother had taken off the market so Kelley could go home to it when she was well. Her mother, her sister, her cat, and EO. That was all she *really* needed, if you got right down to it.

Kelley reached down the bed for the Scrabble game. She thought about the Phantom of the Opera writing his dark music for the night. All he ever wanted was to be loved by someone. She took the cover off the Scrabble game and lifted the board. Her mother caught this out of the corner of her eye and tried to finish up.

Slowly, Kelley stirred the square wooden letters with her left hand. She knew it was time to open the door deep inside. One by one, she drew seven letters and stood them up on a little wooden rack.

Her mother folded up her telephone and put it away. She didn't say anything, just picked out her letters and quickly arranged them.

"Your turn, Kelley. You go first," she said.

Yes. Kelley knew it was her turn.

Her turn and *still* she didn't say anything! She played a whole game of Scrabble and never said a word. Even when her mother hugged her and told her at the end, "I can't come tomorrow. I have two closings, one in the morning and one late afternoon."

Funny, how you can't even figure yourself sometimes. Pathetic actually.

Kelley shook her head after her mother left, pressed her wrists to the plastic on her forehead, and leaned into it hard, until it hurt. This was all so stupid. She knew it, and yet she felt trapped by her own anger. Stymied by indecision! It was as though there were two Kelleys now: one who blamed and one who needed. They were two different people and they were one.

Maybe, Kelley decided, that was her goal: to figure out who she was now because she wasn't the same old Kelley Anne Brennan anymore. And never would be.

# *ten*

A ROOMMATE ARRIVED THE NEXT DAY. They had no choice, Kelley was told. The burn unit was full and so was pediatrics. Kelley had always thought this would bother her, but now she didn't care. She didn't care much about anything, in fact. It didn't matter who they stuck in the room with her.

Still, a roommate was hard to ignore, and this one was so little, only two years old. The name on her chart said simply "Ruby D." because for a while no one knew her last name, only that it began with a *D*. So the nurses started calling her Ruby D., which in Kelley's mind became Ruby Dee.

Even with the curtain pulled between their beds, Kelley could hear the nurses talking about her.

"There is no mother, no, and they can't track down the father."

"Didn't intake say there was a sister somewhere?"

"Yeah, I think so. Maybe even in the same foster home."

"Is that where she had the accident?"

"In the kitchen. She reached up and pulled a pot of boiling water off the stove. Scald burn both arms, here and here, second degree. Then mostly first, some second on the legs."

Kelley winced at the mention of second degree, but she was glad it was mostly first on the legs. First degree was relatively minor—like a sunburn at the beach. It hurt, but it got better in a few days.

When they were finished, the nurses pushed back the curtain, and Kelley pretended she was asleep. Then, after they left, she rolled her head to look at Ruby Dee. The baby was asleep in a crib that stood on high legs, with a plastic covering over the top so a child couldn't climb out. Kelley thought the crib looked like an animal cage the way it was enclosed, and up high.

"Poor Ruby," Leslie whispered soon after as she pulled on her plastic gloves and prepared to check Kelley's leg. She must have known that Kelley wondered about her little roommate even though she still wasn't saying anything.

"Sad to say," Leslie went on, "but children like Ruby are the most frequent patients we see up here. Kids coming from homes where there might be five or six siblings—brothers and sisters—and little or no supervision.

It usually happens in the kitchen. Something hot gets spilled. Someone touches the stove or a burner on the stove."

Leslie finished rubbing some ointment on Kelley's leg and pulled her plastic gloves off with a snap. "Lookin' good," she announced brightly. "Do you remember that the pins are coming out this afternoon?"

Kelley gave a subtle nod. How could she forget something as important as that? Now that the infection was under control, a final skin graft was being planned, too. She would have the surgery in a day or two. Then, maybe, she would actually go home.

Leslie patted Kelley's hand. "Big day for you. I'll see you later."

After Leslie left, a nurse came and took Ruby Dee to the tub room. Kelley had never been to the tub room because of her broken leg and her need to stay in bed, but she knew by now how most burn patients were gently lowered into a tub of warm water for debridement, the removal of dead skin. Kelley wondered how they would do this with a baby, but since Kelley wasn't talking, she couldn't ask.

"Kelley, look at me," Leslie ordered.

Kelley always turned her head away when they gave her an injection. But now that the local anesthetic had been given, she focused on Leslie, who stood with her hands on her hips while Dr. Brewer pulled his surgical gloves on.

"This is going to be over so fast, you won't believe it," Leslie told her.

"Leslie is right," Dr. Brewer said, peering over his glasses at Kelley. "I'm just going to unscrew the pins and slide them out. You must be a brave girl and stay very still."

"Don't listen to him," Leslie joked. "You don't have to be all that brave, Kelley. Here's what I'd do: When he pulls, you and I, we'll holler: 'One, two, three, oh, my God! Can you scream louder than me?' "

Kelley had to hide the smirk that was sneaking onto her face. Of course she wouldn't call out. Instead, she squeezed her eyes tight and gripped the edges of the examining table.

Leslie did it for her: "One, two, three, oh, my God! Can you scream louder than me?" And one pin was out.

Five more times and it was over. In less than half an hour, the whole procedure was finished. The pins that had held her leg bone together for eight weeks were gone.

After the anesthetic wore off, her leg was a little sore, but there was a new feeling of lightness to it. Kelley began to imagine walking all the way down the driveway at home to get the mail or ambling through the wide corridors at the mall.

Later, Kelley was allowed to take her first shower. Although she had to sit on a chair in the shower because she was still weak, she stayed for nearly twenty minutes anyway, soaping and resoaping, rinsing and rerinsing. When dinner came, Kelley discovered she had an appetite. Baked chicken, mashed potatoes, salad, chocolate cake. It all tasted good.

It was after visiting hours, after the evening snack, that Ruby began to cry. Kelley tried reading and listening to her music, but nothing could drown out Ruby's whimpering.

"Hey, there! Ruby Dee Dee! Look at me, me!" Different nurses came to fix the baby's blanket, wiggle a hand puppet in her face, or give her a bottle of juice. But as soon as they left, Ruby started in again.

Finally, when the lights were dimmed for the night and still Ruby cried, Kelley took her earphones off. She knew what the baby needed. She hesitated and cast an angry glance toward the doorway because it wasn't her job. Disgusted, Kelley threw off her covers and reached for her crutches.

"Shhhhhh," she whispered as she maneuvered her way across the short distance between beds to sit in a chair beside the crib. "It's okay."

Ruby was turned toward the doorway and lay on her side, holding the slats of her crib. Kelley reached into the crib with her left hand, the one without a glove, to stroke Ruby Dee's small furrowed brow. "It's okay," she repeated quietly.

At the sound of her voice and the touch of her hand, the baby stopped crying and turned to look at Kelley. In the dim light that seeped into the room from around a door left slightly ajar, they were able to see each other. Kelley smiled at Ruby Dee from inside the mask and couldn't help but wonder: Did she see a face first? Was she scared?

The baby rolled over toward Kelley. Her plastic diaper crinkled, the only sound in the quiet room, and her small wet fingers reached out to curl around Kelley's thumb.

"Hey, I know it hurts," Kelley said. "I've been there, too."

Ruby Dee's wet eyes grew wide.

"The first few days are the hardest. Well, they say they are, anyway. I'm not so sure. But the pain does kind of fade away after a while. Then what you need to do is focus on your goal—of getting better."

Kelley knew the baby didn't understand. But she remembered how the sound of Leslie's voice had once comforted her. So she told Ruby Dee all about the great blue heron back at Loblolly Point and how her pony's hair got all thick and fuzzy, like a teddy bear, in the winter.

In just a few minutes, Ruby was asleep, her fingers wrapped around Kelley's. Gently, Kelley started to lift them off, then thought better of it and laid her head down against her arm. Just a minute or two, she figured, until she was sure Ruby was asleep.

Kelley closed her eyes, too, and a strange, warm feeling spread into her limbs. Gently, she moved her leg without the pins back and forth beneath the chair. Deep inside, the door had been unbolted. Kelley felt the lift as it swung open.

# eleven

"GOOD MORNING," KELLEY SAID TO Leslie the next morning.

Leslie stopped writing on her clipboard and spun around. "What did you say?"

Kelley dropped her eyes. "You heard me."

Leslie beamed. "Kelley Anne Brennan!" She set the clipboard down and hugged Kelley.

"Sorry I acted like such a jerk," Kelley mumbled. Although she was not totally sorry for her silence. She was still going to retreat from the world.

Leslie put a hand on Kelley's shoulder. "Don't be sorry. When you go through something this traumatic, Kelley, emotions and feelings get all mixed up. It's not easy to sort through everything all at once."

She looked up at Leslie. "I do feel confused," she said.

"So just take it one step at a time, okay? Don't be so hard on yourself. Recovery is not a smooth, straight road. There are going to be a lot of bumps, a lot of ups and downs along the way. Do you know that old saying, 'Two steps forward, one step back'?"

Kelley nodded and folded the edge of her sheet.

"I've been having bad dreams," she said. "Nightmares, sometimes."

"That doesn't surprise me, Kelley."

"But these are real nightmares, Leslie. I mean that they might be *real*."

"Oh?"

Kelley hesitated briefly. "I daydreamed—or I thought I remembered, I don't know which—that my mother, well, that we were in the car and that I could see the whole accident, the whole entire thing. And it scares me what I saw."

"Nightmares after a trauma like yours are very common, Kelley. You mustn't let them scare you."

"But do you think the dreams are real? The way it *really* happened?"

Leslie shrugged. "Maybe. But probably not."

Kelley wasn't sure she wanted to say anything more, especially if Leslie didn't think the nightmare was real. She glanced at the clock, wondering what time it was in Europe because there was something else she needed to do.

Her mother came soon afterward and was so happy to hear Kelley talking again, her eyes got all watery. She had brought tuna fish sandwiches and vanilla milk shakes with her so they could have lunch together.

When they finished eating, Kelley suggested they call Leah.

"Kelley! It is so good to hear your voice again!" her sister exclaimed. "Did you get my package?"

"Package?"

"The art things—the pastels. You said you were drawing a lot."

"I think so. Yes. Yes, I did," Kelley answered, vaguely remembering that she had Leslie put them somewhere. "I forgot."

"Oh." Leah sounded disappointed.

"Leah, you need to do something for me," Kelley said quickly.

"Anything, Kel. You name it."

Kelley paused. She was thinking about how much she would really like Leah to come home. Leah would understand about the mask and the gloved hand and the weak leg. They could work on these things together. Instead, Kelley mustered her strength and said, "Don't come."

She repeated it. "Don't come home, Leah. I don't want you to miss your trip because of me."

Quickly, she handed the phone back to her mother.

"You don't have a choice, Leah. You'll upset her terribly if you come back." Her mother explained it better. Her mother made it final.

. . .

After her mother left, Ruby began to cry again, and Kelley found herself at the little girl's bedside with Mr. Potato Head in her hands. Soon it became a game. Kelley would put Mr. Potato Head together, then Ruby Dee would pull out his nose and stick a tongue in the nose hole instead. Kelley would shake her head and say, "You're crazy!" and Ruby Dee would giggle and make Kelley do it all over— again and again.

It didn't last long, however. A quietness settled over Kelley. Suddenly, she didn't want to play Mr. Potato Head anymore because deep inside, even this seemingly innocent game had begun to hurt. It was true, Kelley realized. She was a freak, too—just like Mr. Potato Head with his tongue in his nose hole.

*The road to recovery is not a straight one.* Leslie's words came back to her. Is this what it was going to be like? Kelley stared at the floor, wondering how she would ever go forward.

*"For she WAS a jolly good patient!*
*She WAS a jolly good patient!*
*She WAS a jolly good pa-eeee-tient! That nobody can deny!"*

Six nurses sang and paraded into Kelley's room four nights later, holding candles and circling her bed.

It was time to say good-bye.

They brought with them a chocolate Sara Lee cake from the ABC, still a little frozen, ice-cream cups, a surgical glove filled with M&M's, and one small gift: a new pair of pierced earrings—tiny, shiny green frogs similar to the ones Kelley had lost in the accident. Kelley examined the earrings with a pained expression, not only because of the memory they conjured but because Leslie knew the earring holes had closed up.

Leslie seemed to know what she was thinking. She put an arm around Kelley and leaned close. "So you go to the mall one day with your friends, to one of those jewelry stores, and you get your ears re-pierced. It's no big deal."

Uncertain about this, Kelley closed the little box and mumbled, "Thanks."

"A toast to the leg!" Leslie proposed, raising a cup of iced Sprite over the newly grafted skin on Kelley's right leg.

"A toast to Kelley!" Anita sang out.

"Here! Here!"

Teary-eyed now, Kelley tried to smile back at them. How could she ever thank these people?


All that time, eight long weeks, and suddenly, the moment was upon her. Sitting in a wheelchair in the elevator, Kelley watched the heavy metal doors close and knew that while a chapter in her life was ending, the story had a long way to go. There was a clunk, and the elevator stopped with a jerk.

When the doors opened, the people waiting to enter stood aside. Kelley's mother pushed the wheelchair out into the lobby. An aide was behind them, carrying a box of plants and a duffel bag full of Kelley's clothes. Kelley felt tight inside. She touched the edge of her mask and cowered inside it, avoiding the eyes of the people they passed by looking straight ahead or down at the floor.

At the front door, a woman impatiently urged two young children to enter. But one of her little ones had spotted Kelley and stood, staring at her while holding a doll, limp, in her hand. Kelley caught the small eyes briefly, and saw the look of uncertainty. A mask first. There was no question about it.

"Come on, come *on!*" she heard the woman exclaim. "It's not polite to stare!"

Kelley's mother pushed on a little faster, bumping roughly through the front doors. Outside, the sun was painfully bright. Even with a hat on, Kelley had to squint. When they got to the car, Kelley saw her huge stuffed Dalmatian sitting in the backseat like an extra passenger beside boxes and paper bags full of books, magazines, and other stuffed animals.

After settling herself up front, Kelley looked back at the hospital entrance and ached, suddenly, because she hadn't said good-bye to Ruby Dee. She had been in the tub room when Kelley left. What would happen to Ruby? she wondered. No one, not a single person except a social worker from Baltimore County, had ever come to visit Ruby Dee in the few days she shared a room with Kelley.

Her mother slammed the car's trunk and started to climb in beside her.

"Mom, wait," Kelley said. "I want to give that dog— that big dog—to Ruby Dee."

"The Dalmatian?"

Kelley nodded.

"Your father gave it to you."

"I know. But what am I going to do with it?"

Her mother thought about this and shrugged. "Okay." She called the aide over and explained. "For the little girl in Kelley's room."

The aide opened the back door and maneuvered the stuffed animal out. She leaned toward the front window. "It's really nice of you," she said to Kelley. "Good luck."

"Thanks," Kelley replied quietly.

Her mother started the engine. They were right where they were two months ago, Kelley couldn't help but think. She felt something catch in her throat.

"You were there a long time," her mother said, reaching over to squeeze Kelley's left hand. "We'll take it easy. Don't be afraid."

Her mother withdrew her hand and slowly pulled away from the curb. Kelley turned to look out the side window again. She saw the aide approaching the front entrance of the hospital with the big Dalmatian, then she looked up and tried to find her floor by counting windows. But they had turned a corner, and suddenly the hospital was behind them.

# twelve

KELLEY'S EYES FLICKED OPEN IN the half-light of early dawn. She could feel her heart pounding. Something had frightened her. A nightmare? Was she reliving the accident again? It came once more. A *sound*—a sharp sound mixed with the cool morning air seeping through a screened window. Suddenly, Kelley realized—remembered—that this was the harsh squawk of a great blue heron. *Her* great blue heron!

Relieved and excited, Kelley sat up to listen and felt a strange weight shift beside her leg. At the touch of her hand, Tigger rolled onto his side, stretched his four legs, and began to purr. Kelley took in a deep breath and gently stroked the back of his head. A small cat, purring beside her knees. Proof that she was home again.

She looked around, amazed all over again at how the

guest room had been transformed into her room because she couldn't manage all the stairs to the second floor. Everything was here—her desk, her books from school, the pictures on the walls, her wooden clothes tree blooming with her hat collection. Her mother had even draped her pink feather boa over the top edge of the opened closet door, exactly the way Kelley had arranged it upstairs.

On the nightstand by her bed, the digits on her clock radio glowed 6:00 A.M. Right about now, the night shift would be leaving, Kelley thought. She couldn't help but still feel the rhythm of hospital life. Someone would have been in soon to take her blood pressure and click the temperature gun in her ear.

Had she really been there for two months?

The ride home yesterday seemed like a blur to her now. Her mother, apologizing for the used car she had bought. But the car was fine. Kelley didn't care. Outside, on Eastern Avenue, storefronts and gas stations flashed by. A large bus roared past, spewing black exhaust, and when it cleared, Kelley saw a man without legs in a wheelchair, trying to open the door to a small grocery store.

"Go ahead, turn the radio on," her mother had urged.

Kelley leaned forward and tuned in her favorite station, then lowered the volume.

"Mrs. Peterson made you a blueberry pie," her mother said. "Oh, and Julianna came over yesterday and gave EO a bath. She cleaned out his stall, too. She wanted him to smell like a rose when you got home."

"Ah, I can't wait to see him," Kelley said.

When her mother stopped the car to pay the toll at the Fort McHenry Tunnel, the pause had elicited a momentary, eerie sense of déjà vu. It occurred to Kelley then that she had never once heard her mother describe what *she* remembered about the accident. But on the other hand, Kelley had asked everyone not to talk about it. So it wasn't like her mother was *hiding* anything.

Was it?

As they descended through the tunnel beneath the Patapsco River, the radio reception disappeared, and they rode the darkened length in silence.

When they emerged into daylight, the station returned. Kelley turned up the music and looked out the window toward the city of Baltimore. She recognized the huge baseball stadium at Camden Yards. People at the hospital had been talking about the game scheduled there that night. Dr. Brewer was taking his teenage son. The Orioles were playing the New York Yankees.

Kelley had been to lots of Orioles games because Alison's father had season tickets. They were box seats on the lower deck behind third base. At the games, Kelley and Alison pigged out on nachos and took turns with the binoculars watching Brady Anderson in center field. Alison thought he was really cute. They jumped up out of their seats to do the "wave." Thousands of people would fill that stadium tonight to jump and cheer and eat peanuts. And not one of them, Kelley thought, would be wearing a plastic face mask.

Her mother had turned down the radio. "I don't want you worrying about schoolwork right away," she said.

"Leslie told me there's a tutor coming," Kelley responded without turning to look at her.

"Yes! Yes, there is. She's *wonderful*. I know you'll like her."

Kelley thought her mother was sounding a little too gung ho.

"There's a lot of work to make up, but she'll help. So don't feel overwhelmed."

Kelley didn't say anything.

"After all, you've got the whole summer to make it up."

Already—they were not even halfway home—Kelley had felt herself slipping. A heavy, helpless feeling tugged at her inside. Her mother's words echoed in her head—*a lot of work to make up*—as the car wound around a cloverleaf and merged into a different stream of traffic. But Kelley told herself she didn't care about the work she had missed because she had no intention of making it up.

Kelley had decided she was not going back to school. It was part of the Grand Plan she had made the moment those Velcro straps were pulled taut against the back of her head. She shuddered to think of the kids in her class who would turn away, gasping and clasping their hands over their mouths. She didn't think they would be juvenile or cruel enough to call her names. But she knew the hypocritical, sweet-voiced girls who would smile and say, "Oh, Kelley, it's so nice to have you back," then turn around and be grossed out by the mask and the way she looked.

Kelley figured if she dragged out the makeup work long enough, she could convince her mother she needed to stay home. She had met a girl in her ballet class who studied at home through a computer program. Staying home was the only answer. If plastic surgery down the road helped her, then fine. Maybe she could go back to school one day. But not until then.

Kelley stared at her bureau and, gradually, the framed pictures upon it came into focus: Leah with a toothy grin, holding a rose in her teeth on graduation day; another of Kelley and Liesel, their arms draped around poor Alison, who had broken her arm Rollerblading.

It wasn't so long ago that she and Alison and Liesel stood before the mirror over that bureau, experimenting with clips in their hair and trying out different lipsticks and eye shadows, dabbing glittery body gel on their cheeks. With each stunning application they would blow kisses and flirt with their own reflections, then stick out their tongues and fall back on the bed laughing.

Now, like a stage curtain closing the show, a white towel was draped over the mirror. It seemed out of place, hastily arranged, as did the sheet, thumbtacked to the inside of the closet door, where there was a full-length mirror. Her mother had refused to let her cover the mirrors elsewhere in the house, but she agreed, finally, that Kelley had a right to do it in her own room.

Kelley lay back down, pulling the covers up to her chin. But it was no use trying to sleep anymore. She was wide awake. And she was home! Things were supposed to be different now. She would take a shower, she decided. Get a clean, fresh start on the first day home.

Stepping into her terry-cloth slippers, she grabbed the crutches that leaned against the footrail of her bed and made her way down the hall to the bathroom. She started the shower and undressed while the water warmed up. When it was the right temperature, she entered, turning her face into the hard stream of water and letting it pummel her scars. She never stopped wishing that the water would wash away the grotesque red patches on her face, leaving her old self there instead. That's all she wanted— her simple, plain, old self back. She did not care about "pretty" anymore, just a cheek with freckles to match the other cheek, an eyebrow with a few hairs in it, a forehead that wrinkled all the way across.

The trip home yesterday flashed into her mind again. Kelley, sitting in the passenger seat, tightening up as the intersection approached. She had dreaded seeing it again. Her mother must have known. She was quiet, focused on her driving. Kelley thought about closing her eyes when the time came but didn't, just stared out the window and squeezed her right wrist so hard it made her hand fall asleep.

Suddenly they were at the intersection—Kelley felt her chest get tight—but there was nothing there. *Nothing!* Not a single reminder of the accident. No broken glass or crumpled sheets of metal. No skid marks or spilled lumber from Quentin Hall's truck. Just a traffic signal hanging motionless above the road with a solid green light. Like nothing had ever happened.

*Nothing.*

*Ever.*

And yet, here she was, Kelley Anne Brennan, changed for life.

The water beat hard and became hotter. Kelley continued to face into it, letting the tears come, as she always did, because all thoughts came back to this eventually. Even on her first day home, when things were supposed to be different. Maybe every day of the rest of her life would start this way, Kelley thought. It would be a ritual, something she had to do first. Cry. *Cry and get it over with.* Then pick up the soap and move on.

# thirteen

As she sat on the edge of her bed, combing out her wet hair, Kelley heard noises coming from the kitchen: pots being banged around, the oven door opening and closing, a timer going off. Soon, the smell of fresh-baked blueberry muffins made its way back to Kelley's room and lured her out.

"Good morning," her mother greeted her cheerfully. Already dressed, she was putting the hot muffins into a basket, which she set on a kitchen table decked out with a vase of bright yellow daylilies and crisp blue place mats. "How did you sleep?"

"Pretty good," Kelley said. "I almost forgot where I was when I woke up."

Her mother gave her a hug, then took her crutches

and pulled out a chair for her. "Well, you're home," she said. "And you get the royal treatment. I'll make anything you want: bacon, eggs, Irish oatmeal. You name it."

Kelley chose scrambled eggs, which her mother made with shredded cheddar cheese and served with muffins and a big glass of orange juice. "We need to get some meat back on those bones," her mother kept saying. Kelley had lost fifteen pounds, and all of her clothes did seem to hang on her.

As she always did, Kelley took off her mask to eat. "This is so good, Mom," she said. "Especially the eggs. Did you know at the hospital they made their eggs out of cardboard?"

"Kelley—"

"It's true!" Kelley paused to scoop up Tigger, who was rubbing up against her chair. "Boy, I missed you," she murmured into his fur.

It was understood that today would be a slow day, a day of adjustment for Kelley. Which is why she was a little perturbed when her mother said she heard someone coming up the driveway.

"I really don't want to see anyone. Not today," Kelley insisted.

"But it's just Helen," her mother said as she peered out the window over the kitchen sink.

Helen Peterson was a neighbor and a good friend of Kelley's mom. She was also a terrific cook and had made the blueberry pie they ate last night.

"I'm sure she won't be long," Kelley's mother said. "She said yesterday she wanted to drop something off in the morning, and I couldn't say no. Please, Kelley, she's been such a help to me."

Kelley sighed.

"I'm sure she'll understand," her mother said.

"Okay—it's all right." Kelley gave in.

She continued eating while her mother went to the door and invited Mrs. Peterson in.

"Oh, my golly. It's so good to see you home, sweetheart," Mrs. Peterson gushed. She set a cake down on the table and hustled over to Kelley to kiss the top of her head.

"I brought you your favorite," she said, indicating the frosted carrot cake.

"It looks delicious," Kelley said.

Mrs. Peterson smiled down at her, but her lips were pressed tight, and Kelley could see the glistening in her eyes.

"Helen, we really enjoyed your pie last night. Didn't we, Kelley?" her mother asked.

"Umm, we did," Kelley agreed.

"How about a cup of coffee?" Kelley's mother asked.

"No, no, I don't think so," Mrs. Peterson said. "I won't stay but a minute."

But a minute became ten, and Kelley noticed how Mrs. Peterson never looked back at her again. Not once. Was it because she didn't want Kelley to see her tears? Or because she couldn't bear to look anymore?

Kelley put her fork down and stared at the plastic face mask on the table beside her.

. . .

"I want to see my pony," Kelley said after Mrs. Peterson left.

"All right. I can handle that," Kelley's mother agreed. "Why don't you wait on the back steps? It might be a little too far for you to go on crutches just yet—or I can go get that wheelchair we borrowed."

"That's okay. I'll let you bring him up. I just want to say 'hi.'"

While her mother went down to the barn to fetch EO, Kelley found a box of Froot Loops and sat on the back steps waiting.

"Hey! Long time no see!" she greeted her old friend as he clomped up the driveway and clip-clopped over the sidewalk.

EO went straight to her hand.

"First things first, huh?" Kelley teased, letting him sweep the cereal from her hand.

"He looks so clean," her mother said.

"And feels so soft," Kelley noted, patting his neck.

EO lifted his nose up toward Kelley's chin.

"I missed you, too," she said.

After EO was taken back, Kelley picked up her crutches and hobbled through the house to the deck, where she settled into a lounge chair. The cool morning air was gone, replaced by humidity that was already beginning to bear down. Long sleeves and pants didn't help, but it would be important, she was told repeatedly, to cover up the burn areas from the sun, especially her face. So even in the shade of a patio umbrella, Kelley pulled her baseball cap on.

She leaned her head back and closed her eyes. Above her, high in the sycamore branches, the cicadas buzzed, and far off, a boat's motor churned as it came up the creek from the bay. The sounds of summer, she thought. The accident had happened at the end of April, but now it was early July. She had missed an entire season.

Not only was spring gone, but so were Alison and Liesel. Liesel was off to summer camp in Maine while Alison had gone to the Outer Banks of North Carolina, where she was a mother's helper to four-year-old twins. Each of them had been writing faithfully, their letters filled with gossip and news. Alison—so relentlessly cheerful even after the way Kelley had treated her in the hospital. She had never once mentioned it in her letters.

Kelley's eyes grew misty. Alison with her dimples and her silly jokes: *What lies at the bottom of the ocean and shakes?* she had asked Kelley in her wide, swirling cursive. *A nervous wreck! That's what Tyler and Brett have made me—and I've only been here a week!* And poor Liesel, listening to loons and learning how to shoot a bow and arrow. What good was that going to do her?

They were good friends. There was no question about it. And yet, the last two letters from Alison and Liesel lay unopened, in a packet of papers Kelley brought home from the hospital. She put them in the basket beneath her nightstand with all the Get Well cards and To Cheer You notes from still others who hadn't given up on her.

There was a whole pile of letters, unopened, from the kids in her class. Odd how they all came during the last week of school. A class assignment? She could just hear

Mrs. Scherpa in English class: *All right, people, listen up! Let's all write one more note to poor Kelley before we leave for the summer.* Ha! If they only knew she hadn't bothered to read their stupid little patronizing notes.

Kelley twisted her mouth and flicked a ladybug off the arm of her chair. The only letters she read now were from Leah, who was traveling in Italy.

Not that she was too busy to read anything but Leah's letters. Except for the tutor who was coming and appointments at the burn clinic and physical therapy in Baltimore every week, the summer stretched before Kelley like an endless dry desert of time. It would be hard enough trudging across it, but Kelley would have to do it knowing that there was no oasis on the other side. The other side of summer meant a return to school and friends and routines she didn't want anything to do with anymore.

Even Alison's and Liesel's lives would be different from Kelley's now. They were normal twelve-year-olds. Kelley wouldn't have much in common with them anymore. It was time to let them go.

She would just be by herself. Hiding out. Sticking to the plan. If her mother resisted, all Kelley had to do was look her in the eye and say, "No one with half a face should be forced to go to school."

She hoped she wouldn't have to say any more than that.

Sadly, Kelley bit on her thumbnail and was staring off into the distance when she heard another car coming up the driveway.

"Oh, no," she moaned out loud, frowning and hoping

her mother wouldn't bring whoever it was out back to gawk at her.

"Just leave me alone," she mumbled, cringing at the sound of a car door slamming and her mother's *overly* cheerful greeting.

But then, suddenly, something else carried crisply, clearly, in the still, hot air. Something that made Kelley sit up and suck in her breath. She put a hand to her mouth because yes—*yes it was,* she realized—the sound of Leah's voice!

"Leah!"

"Kelley!"

"I can't believe you're here!"

Leah rushed to embrace her little sister. "Oh, my gosh. I have missed you so much. You just don't know."

Kelley pressed her face and mask into Leah's silk-shirted shoulder. "I missed you, too. But I didn't want you to come home, Leah. You were supposed to stay and see Europe."

Leah took Kelley by the shoulders and gently pushed her back to look into her face. If the mask startled her, she didn't show it. "Europe is not going to go anywhere," she said. "I can see it another time. With *you,* maybe."

Beautiful Leah. Everything about her was still so perfect: her smooth blond hair, her confident smile, her bright green eyes. Kelley watched those eyes study her face as Leah's smile faded.

"I am so sorry this happened to you," she said.

Kelley nodded. "I know."

"But I'm home. And I want to help, Kelley." She perked up again. "Did Mom tell you? I'm your tutor!"

Astonished, Kelley looked at her mother, who was standing behind Leah with a sheepish grin. Her mother shrugged and held up her hands. "You would have thrown a fit if we told you. Leah insisted on returning home, Kelley. She was coming back regardless of what we said."

"That's right. Once I made up my mind I took the first plane I could get. And that was the flight last night—out of Rome," Leah said. She widened her eyes and leaned toward Kelley. "Nine hours on that plane to New York and guess what the movie was?"

Kelley shrugged.

"A Rugrats movie."

"Oh, no." Kelley rolled her eyes.

"Hold on to your diapees!!" Leah exclaimed, mimicking the cartoon toddler star. "They showed it *twice,* too. I mean, what were they thinking? Oh, well. I had a very nice man sitting beside me. He told me all about his grandchildren, gave me excellent advice on the stock market. And if we ever get to Minneapolis, we're to look him up." Leah shook her head. "What a chatterbox. At least I got my nails done!"

Kelley glanced at Leah's lovely fingernails. "I just can't believe you're here."

"Been a long time," Leah said. "I haven't seen you since Christmas."

Kelley heard the catch in her sister's voice and saw the tears pooling in Leah's eyes.

"Don't cry," Kelley said.

Leah took Kelley's hands, then reached around to hug her again. "Oh, Kelley, you're going to be okay. I know you are."

# fourteen

AFTER LEAH HAD UNPACKED A few things, taken a shower, and changed, she brought gifts to the kitchen table and laid out her plans.

"What I want to do," she said, "is get a part-time job to make money for school, but leave my mornings free to work with Kelley."

"What kind of a job?" her mother asked.

Leah took a long drink of lemonade and wiped her lips with a napkin. "Maybe I could waitress again at Fran O'Brien's in Annapolis. It's close, and I made a ton in tips."

"Or something at the mall," Kelley suggested, still fingering the elegant silk scarf Leah had brought her from Paris.

"You just want me to work at The Gap so you can get clothes on my employees' discount," Leah teased.

Kelley grinned a little.

"Anyway, I'll make a few calls tomorrow and see what I can dredge up." Turning back to Kelley, Leah added, "First, I want to see this drawing scrapbook Mom told me about."

"It's no big deal," Kelley protested.

"No big deal. Kelley, you *never* told me about the mural you did in school, either. You're too modest."

Kelley blushed.

It was wonderful having Leah home again. The next few days were the happiest Kelley had experienced since the accident. Leah spent hours with her, listening, talking, showing her pictures of Europe—and of Antonio, her new Italian boyfriend. Sometimes, they just sat together on the couch and watched a movie while Kelley squeezed the therapy putty in her hand or did her leg exercises. Once, Leah got out the Monopoly game and they played all afternoon.

Leah asked Kelley a couple of questions about the mask, the Jobst glove, and the exercises she had to do for her leg. But they didn't talk about the accident.

Their mother, meanwhile, left early every day to go to work and returned in the evening with special things like steamed crabs and fresh rockfish for dinner. Leah joked that Kelley was going to put those lost fifteen pounds back on in a week because every night they topped off dinner with a slice of Mrs. Peterson's carrot cake, or else sat on the deck with a bowl of Kelley's favorite chocolate chip cookie dough ice cream.

"Well, I found the perfect job!" Leah announced brightly one evening over dinner. It was the first day she had even tried to find work.

But of course, Kelley thought. Her sister never had to work hard at anything.

"Well? What is it?" Kelley asked, putting some chicken salad on her plate.

"A gift shop in Stevensville. You know, the old part of town that's been 'yuppified' with all those little shops and restaurants. It's absolutely perfect because I can either walk or ride my bike, and it's the afternoon shift, so I'll have all morning to help Kelley with her schoolwork."

She tossed a glance at Kelley across the table. "Speaking of which, we haven't even cracked open a book yet or taken a look at what you've got to make up."

Kelley kept eating and nodded. "I'm not worried about it."

"It's probably time, though," her mother commented. "Pass me the rolls, would you, Kelley?"

Kelley handed the basket of rolls to her mother but avoided making eye contact.

"Say, Kel, how about a walk down to the barn after dinner?" Leah asked later as she began to clear the dishes.

Kelley looked at her mother.

"It's okay," she said. "But you'd better take the wheelchair. It's a long way down and back with just the crutches."

When she had finished cleaning up, Leah rolled the wheelchair up to the back kitchen steps and helped Kelley get seated.

It was a bumpy trip down the gravel driveway to the barn. Leah went slowly, however, and Kelley enjoyed being outside. The last couple of days had been so hot, they had spent all their time inside with the air-conditioning on. But now, with the sun beginning to set, the air was almost pleasant.

Leah pushed the wheelchair over the barn's cement floor, pausing outside the tack room to peer in. "You've still got all my trophies on display?"

"Sure," Kelley said. "Why not?"

Leah lifted one of the trophies from off a shelf above EO's saddle. "You never got into this, did you?" she asked.

Kelley shook her head. "No. I just wanted to ride— for fun."

Leah sighed. "It was a ton of work. A lot of waiting around at all those dusty old horse shows. It's funny now, when I look back on it all. It's like everything I did I had to be the best at it, you know?"

"Oh, I *do* know!" Kelley burst out.

Leah looked at her quizzically.

"You were a *very* hard act to follow," Kelley added emphatically. She softened her voice. "And all I ever wanted was to be like you."

Gently, Leah set the trophy back down. "Gosh, Kelley. I don't think I ever realized—"

"It doesn't matter." Kelley waved her hand. She didn't

want her tired, old jealous feelings to spoil Leah's return. *"Really,"* she said. "I don't know why I said that!"

But Leah frowned and seemed quieter as she pushed the wheelchair through the back door of the barn. Outside, they could see EO and the gray horse, Pulsar, grazing in the pasture.

"EO! Hey, EO!" Leah called.

The pony kept eating.

"I think he's losing his hearing," Kelley told her.

So Leah hollered louder: "Hey! Eohippus! You first horse, you! Get your buns over here!"

This time EO lifted his head and looked at them.

"Come *on!*" Leah urged.

Slowly, the pony turned and began plodding toward them, his hooves kicking up small clouds of dust as he crossed a patch of dirt near the fence.

"What a sweetheart you are," Leah murmured, reaching between the bars of the fence to pet him.

Kelley, too, reached out, eager to feel the familiar velvet nose.

"I didn't mean to say anything to hurt your feelings," Kelley said as she straightened the pony's wiry forelock. "I'm so glad you're home, Leah."

"It's okay. It didn't hurt my feelings."

Leah sat on the grass beside the wheelchair and began pulling grass for the pony. "I need to start my new job tomorrow," she said. "When do you want to get started on all that makeup for school?"

Kelley didn't answer the question. "Why do you have

to start work so soon?" she asked instead. "Couldn't you start next week?"

Leah smiled and offered the grass to EO. "I wish I could. But I need the money. Mom needs the money, I should say. She's had a hard time with this real-estate stuff, you know. Has she talked to you about how tough it's been?"

"No," Kelley said.

"Well, I probably shouldn't say this, but she's a lousy real-estate agent."

"What do you mean?" Kelley asked.

Leah shrugged. "I don't know why, but she's not selling anything—not enough, anyway. But don't you notice something about her, Kelley? She's not the same. You have a conversation with her and it's like she's on another planet, she's so distracted."

Kelley tried to envision the way her mother had been, but it was difficult because her mother was either at work, rushing around doing chores, or making phone calls. Kelley had so many problems of her own, she honestly hadn't noticed.

"I asked her last night if she was still seeing that stock-broker guy, what's his name?"

"Mike?" Kelley asked.

"Mike, yes. She said she didn't have time for him anymore. I don't get it! I mean, she really liked him a few months ago."

It suddenly hit Kelley that she hadn't once thought about Mike at all over the past two months. Hadn't once asked about him or wondered why he never came to the hospital. He was a nice enough person, although Kelley had never gotten to know him very well.

"I don't know what's with her," Leah continued. She plucked a long piece of grass and ran it through her fingers. "Something's not right."

Why *was* her mother distracted? Kelley stared at the back of Leah's head.

"Leah," she said. "What did Mom tell you about the accident?"

"What do you mean?" Leah turned to look at her.

Kelley examined her fingernails. "What did she tell you about how it happened? I'm just curious."

"Well, she told me how it was a dark and rainy night. About the exit and all. The guy with the truck. She doesn't remember the impact—or the seconds right before it. Only that when she came to and smelled the gas, she knew you had to get out before the car exploded. She said it all happened so fast."

"What about the guy in the truck? What happened to him?"

"Quentin Hall?"

"Yeah, him." Kelley didn't even like saying his name.

"No one ever told you?"

"I never asked," Kelley said.

"No. I don't blame you. I think Mom said he got a broken collarbone and a concussion. Something may have happened to his eyes. . . . What a creep. Don't think about him, Kelley."

A concussion? So maybe Quentin Hall couldn't remember anything, either, Kelley suddenly realized. If what she remembered was real, then maybe she was the only one who knew the truth! She frowned, thinking once again how it couldn't possibly have happened. Not *really*. But how would she ever know?

Leah misread the expression on Kelley's face.

"I'm sorry, Kelley! I shouldn't have worried you so much about Mom. You have enough problems. I'm sure Mom's just worried because she loves you so much."

Kelley smiled faintly and nodded with a faraway look in her eyes. "I'm sure."

# fifteen

THE NEXT MORNING KELLEY COULD see what her sister meant.

It was just after breakfast. Her mother was putting the cereal bowls into the dishwasher, rushing because she was late for work. Kelley sat at the table, fixing a cup of tea.

"Leah and I can do that," she said. "We can clean up."

But her mother continued.

"What time will you be home tonight, Mom?" Kelley asked.

Her mother had stopped to scrape something off the rim of a glass. "Usual time, I guess," she said.

"We thought, Leah and I, that maybe we could all play Monopoly tonight."

"Sure," her mother replied. She poured dish detergent into the dishwasher.

"Listen, Mom. If you want, you could go out some night. Now that Leah's home, you don't have to worry about being here all the time." Kelley stirred her tea. "I mean it," she said. "You and Mrs. Peterson could go to the movies or out to dinner like you used to. Remember? Moms' night out?"

Kelley paused while her mother closed the dishwasher door. "Or you could go out on a date." She paused. "With Mike maybe."

Her mother started the machine and was wiping her hands on a towel.

"What do you think?" Kelley asked.

She smiled at Kelley. "Monopoly? Sure."

And Kelley realized she'd lost her halfway through the conversation.

Okay, so what was it? Kelley tried to figure. Work? That guy Mike? Or was it something she hadn't even thought of yet? Maybe something the doctors had told her mother that they hadn't told Kelley? In fact, there was a message on the answering machine from a doctor Kelley had never heard of before—a Dr. Hoffberg. Dr. Lillian Hoffberg. Kelley didn't pay much attention. But now she wondered: Who the heck was that? Was there yet another complication she didn't know about?

Two days later Kelley was still dwelling on it when she set down the drawing she had been working on and stretched out on the couch. Leah had gone to work, her second day on the job, and Kelley was alone. She picked up the bag of therapy putty and squeezed it hard.

Suddenly, she heard the back door unlock. Sitting up,

she cleared her throat. She had practiced what to say: *Mom, I have this funny feeling. I mean, you're here but you're not here. Is there something you haven't told me?*

Her mother came into the room and set her briefcase down. Her mascara had smudged a little, probably from all the heat, and she did look tired. Her whole face kind of sagged. It occurred to Kelley then that maybe her mother was just plain tired.

"Hi, sweetie," she said, breaking into a smile and coming over to kiss the top of Kelley's head. "Is this Tigger?" She picked up the drawing Kelley had been working on earlier. "It's wonderful! Really, Kelley, it's *very* good."

And Kelley knew she couldn't ask what was wrong.

It made her angry that she was so weak. When her mother left the room, she tore up the picture she'd been working on. Frustrated, she crossed her arms and stared at the ceiling until her mother came back and coaxed her outside.

"Let's set you up under this tree," her mother said, carrying a folding chair and Kelley's backpack to a shady spot.

Kelley followed slowly on her crutches.

Her mother opened up the chair. "Maybe being out here will inspire you."

Kelley handed her the crutches and carefully sat down.

Her mother gazed off toward the water and already seemed lost in other thoughts. "Peaceful, isn't it?"

Peaceful? Kelley summoned her courage. "Mom, what is it you're not telling me?"

Surprised, her mother turned. "What do you mean?"

"Is there something the doctors said that you haven't told me?"

"No. Absolutely not," her mother replied, shaking her head. "Kelley, there is nothing the doctors have said that we haven't told you."

"Then who is Dr. Hoffberg?"

Her mother was startled and almost stuttered. "D-Dr. Hoffberg? What do you mean?"

"There was a message on the answering machine. To call her office."

"Oh." Her mother seemed greatly relieved. "Yes, I need to call her. I've had a problem with my, ah—my leg. You know, where I was cut and had stitches? Maybe the muscle or something. I get spasms there. Nothing to worry about."

Kelley studied her mother; she wasn't sure she believed this.

"But you *seem* so worried all the time. Even Leah noticed. She said you were distracted."

"She did?" Her mother pondered this, then knelt beside Kelley's chair. "Well, I am worried," she said. "About our finances, mostly. In fact, one reason Leah came home is that I couldn't afford to hire a tutor all summer. She's even offered to take a semester off to work. But I'd hate to have her do that.

"I don't know," her mother continued. "Maybe I'm not cut out for this work. Sales are picking up a little, though. Your father's helped out some. Things will be okay. I don't want you to worry about it." She squeezed Kelley's left hand.

But Kelley was not convinced. She looked into her mother's eyes, waiting for more.

"Now." Her mother lifted her eyebrows. "There is something I need to ask *you*. Alison called me today at the office."

Kelley had been afraid this would come up. She sighed and turned away.

"She said she tried to get you at home the last two afternoons, but no one answered."

When Kelley didn't say anything, her mother continued. "She also said the answering machine was not on. Kelley, I don't understand why you're shutting out your best friends. This is the second time Alison has called from Duck. That's a long-distance call from North Carolina—and you're not even answering the phone?"

Kelley stared into her lap.

"Alison cares, you know. She is *trying* to be your friend. But if you don't open up, you're going to lose her. And Liesel, too. It's hard for her to get to the phone, but last night when she called from camp and you were in your room?" Her mother paused. "I know you weren't really sleeping."

Kelley pressed her lips together and didn't say anything. She had to cut off her friends. She was not part of their world anymore.

Her mother stood waiting, with one hand on Kelley's shoulder. But the silence, too, stood, like a wall between them.

"I should get back to work, set up some appointments for tomorrow." Her mother sighed and looked back toward the house. "I think the Nemans are getting ready to buy that big brick colonial up near Love Point, and I said I'd line up the financing."

Kelley knew she should have said something like "Great, you'll get a nice commission," or even "Congratulations." But she did not.

"We need the money," her mother said.

She did not have to repeat it.

"I wish I could take the afternoons off to be with you," her mother said. "But I just can't afford to do it."

"I understand," Kelley said. She knew why her mother worked so hard. She worked hard so Leah and Kelley could have everything they wanted. It was her mother who stayed late at work almost every day in Annapolis so that Kelley could take ballet and piano lessons, be on the field-hockey team, or go to basketball and lacrosse games. It was her mother who had handed over her charge card whenever Kelley needed new shoes or clothes. Her mother who had taken Kelley, Alison, and Liesel to New York City on the train for Kelley's twelfth birthday last February.

And *never to be forgotten:* It was her mother who burned one of her own hands reaching through the window to pull Kelley out after the engine caught fire, mere seconds before the entire car burst into flames.

Kelley looked up at her mother, who was glancing at her watch. Her mother didn't even have a social life because all she did was take care of Kelley and work—even on the weekends.

She had to turn away then, to poke her little finger into the left eyehole of her mask and scoop out the moisture that was forming there. God, she hated to cry with this stupid face mask on. The tears dripped underneath and made her skin all clammy. She had to unstrap it in the back, take it off, rinse it, wipe it out, and redo the whole thing.

"Go ahead, Mom." Kelley sniffed. Her mother didn't notice. "I know you need to make those calls. I'll be okay."

"You're sure?"

Kelley nodded.

"All right, then." Her mother squeezed her shoulders. "I'll come back in a bit and help you in for dinner."

Kelley sat, glumly studying the edge of the marsh and trying to rally enough enthusiasm to start drawing, when, suddenly, two children giggled and popped their heads out of the tall grass.

She suspected right away that they were kids from the new housing development that had sprung up down the road. She put down her pencil and leaned over the arm of her chair to pull the binoculars from her backpack.

The snap and crunch of dried reeds underfoot told her they were coming closer. Kelley swung the binoculars along the water's edge and began to panic. Because what if they came up the hill and saw her?

*Come on, Kelley,* she chided herself. *What's so scary about a couple of little kids? What's the worst they could possibly do? Tie you to your chair? Jump on your poor leg? Steal your crutches?*

No. Nothing like that. Kelley brought the binoculars down. They could come up the hill, the two of them, smiling, and then, all at once, they would stop because they could see. *Really* see. There would be that awkward moment of hesitation and wonder . . . and they would have a choice to make.

Sure, they might try to be brave. But Kelley knew they would be afraid. Grossed out like Mrs. Peterson next door, who couldn't even look at Kelley. Only these kids would scream and run away! She glanced back and saw one of the children running up the hill.

"Mom!" Kelley called out, turning so quickly that she lost her balance and fell off the chair, twisting her leg.

"Help!" she cried as pain shot through her weakened right leg like a bullet. She winced and squeezed her eyes shut, it hurt so bad.

Then it happened. When Kelley opened her eyes, a little girl was slowing to a stop. And the awkward moment of hesitation was upon them.

"I didn't mean to scare you," the little girl said.

*A face first . . .*

Kelley held her breath.

*Then a mask . . .*

The little girl came close. Long black hair flowed to her waist like a cape. She wore an old-fashioned striped dress and pink leather cowboy boots dotted with rhinestones. Their eyes met, and the little girl smiled shyly. A beautiful smile that lit up the dark features of her face.

"Are you okay?" she asked.

# sixteen

THE FIRST THING KELLEY THOUGHT about the next morning was the little girl who hadn't run away. Why hadn't she been scared? Kelley wondered. What did she see? Kelley wished now that her mother hadn't dashed back so quickly and shooed the girl away.

Sitting on the edge of her bed, Kelley pushed the hair out of her face with a headband. Then she took a deep breath and repositioned, then refastened, the mask.

She was having her first official tutoring session with Leah this morning. But she still hadn't completed the two small assignments Leah had asked her to do. Even after breakfast, as she sat on the couch watching a dumb cartoon, Kelley knew there was still time to complete the math paper.

"I'll see you tonight, sweetie," her mother said, kissing the top of her head and breezing out of the room, briefcase in hand.

"See ya," Kelley said, listening to her high heels *tap, tap, tap* down the tile hallway and then disappear with the heavy thud of the front door.

Leah came in soon after with a towel over her shoulders and her hair still wet, but combed out, from a shower. She had on shorts and a baggy T-shirt, a bottle of springwater in one hand and some of Kelley's books in the other. All the books were new. The school had given her mother a whole new set.

"Good morning," she said cheerfully as she sat cross-legged in a soft armchair opposite Kelley.

Kelley toyed with a pencil.

"Okay! You ready?" Leah set the springwater down on the coffee table between them and held the books on her lap. "I've read through all these notes from your teachers. In order to catch up, you have to complete the math book and those last four chapters in science. Plus an English project—it's not too bad. Plus the Spanish workbook, and a section on China in history. Oh, and you need to conclude some sort of an environmental project you started in March."

Kelley looked up at her.

"This is actually a pretty interesting project. Your science teacher wrote that you and three others put up a fence on the roof of the Islander Hardware Store. So the baby least terns wouldn't fall off?" She put the notes down. "You know, Kelley, now that I think of it, you told me about this in a letter, didn't you?"

Kelley nodded meekly while Leah opened a wide envelope full of large, black-and-white photographs. Kelley knew instantly that they were pictures of the tern project. Probably the pictures that Daniel had taken.

"This is so neat!" Leah exclaimed. "I remember now. When you told me, I didn't even know least terns were a threatened species."

She looked at one of the pictures and held it out to Kelley. "You'll have to tell me all about this."

But Kelley wouldn't take the picture. "I don't need to see them," she said.

The smile on Leah's face began to fade. "Yeah." She wrinkled her nose. "You've probably seen all this before. But maybe we could go over someday and—"

"*No!*" Kelley interrupted her. "No way. I am *not* going over there."

"But aren't you curious about how it all turned out?"

"Quite honestly? No!" Kelley laughed. "I am *not* curious."

"Kelley, you headed up this whole project and it was a wonderful idea. Your fence has probably saved hundreds of these birds."

"And so what?" Kelley looked her sister in the eye. "Really, Leah. I mean, who cares about a bunch of stupid terns? Most people don't even know what they are! Little gray birds. Big deal! If they disappear is it going to affect your life? Is it going to affect mine? No! It won't make a lick of difference!"

Kelley looked away.

"All right," Leah said quietly. She piled up the photographs and set them down on the coffee table between them.

Kelley bit on her thumbnail.

"Let's see." Leah reexamined the teachers' notes. "Did you get the math paper done?"

"No," Kelley said.

"How about that first chapter in science?"

Kelley shook her head.

Slowly, Leah tucked the wet hair on one side of her head behind her ear.

"This *is* a lot of work all at once. Why don't we review the science chapter together, to get started?" she suggested.

She took a swig of her springwater and picked out the science book while Kelley reluctantly pulled a notebook onto her lap.

"Chapter Seventeen. Elements." Leah handed Kelley a pen. "Do you remember that an *element* is a pure substance that cannot be broken down?"

Kelley found an empty page, put down the pen, and picked up her pencil.

"When two or more elements are chemically joined together, compounds are formed." Leah emphasized the word *compounds* by glancing up and widening her luminous green eyes. Kelley studied them.

"Organic compounds are basic to life," she explained.

But Kelley did not write this. Instead, she drew a large oval.

"They include carbohydrates, fats and oils, proteins, enzymes, and nucleic acids."

With a quick, sure hand, Kelley sketched in a slender nose and two almond-shaped eyes, lightly shading in the irises.

"Carbohydrates are made from three elements."

She added thick eyelashes and high, arched eyebrows.

"Carbon is one."

Leah's mouth was a little tricky. It was wide, like Julia Roberts's, only her lips were thin and delicate.

"Oxygen is another."

Kelley darkened the lips, then glanced at Leah to discern exactly where her sister's hairline began.

"Do you remember what the third element is?" Leah asked.

With long, loose lines, Kelley began re-creating a head full of thick, wet, hair.

"Kelley."

Kelley stopped drawing.

"Am I going too fast?"

She nodded.

So Leah leaned forward and repeated slowly, "Carbohydrates are made from three elements: carbon, oxygen, and what?"

The eyes defined Leah, Kelley was thinking. The rest of her face was so classically perfect, but the eyes were what set her apart. She would go back to them in a minute.

"What's that third element, Kelley?"

Kelley drew in one hoop earring, then looked up, surprised to see Leah leaning forward and peering over the edge of the notebook.

"I see," she said.

Kelley stopped. "I'm sorry."

"Really, Kelley." Leah stood and came over to see better. "It's very good. You have a nice fluid hand." She cocked her head. "And the eye looks back at you. I don't know that much about drawing. I was never very good at it. But I do know about the eye from that one art class I took last year."

Kelley felt a subtle lurch inside, because without even thinking about it, she had not only drawn an eye but an entire face.

"You do like to draw, don't you?"

Kelley shrugged. "They made me draw in the hospital. For my hand."

"But you enjoyed it."

"I guess."

"Then why not take some art lessons this fall? I can get a catalog from that arts center—Maryland Hall—over in Annapolis, and see what they have." She sat back down. "Or, if you like, I could dig out my notebooks from art class and share some of the stuff I learned."

The idea appealed to Kelley, but she was embarrassed, caught in her act of defiance, and said nothing.

Leah sighed. She was frustrated already, Kelley thought. Maybe realizing that the summer wasn't going to be so hunky-dory after all.

"You don't want to do your schoolwork, do you?" Leah asked.

Kelley rolled the pencil between her fingers.

"Why?" Leah asked. "Is it because it's hard for you to concentrate?"

Kelley frowned, and silently she answered Leah's question. *No, I don't want to do the schoolwork because I am not going back to school!*

"You seem angry, Kelley. Are you angry?"

Her fingers tightened around the pencil. Inside, she felt twisted, confused.

"What is it?"

Kelley's face flushed. Her warm cheeks pressed against the plastic. But no one could see it, could they, because it was all behind the mask?

"Talk to me, Kelley. *Say* something."

Kelley pressed her lips together tightly, then blurted out, "Of course I'm angry!"

Leah threw open her hands. "Why?"

Kelley's eyes flashed. "Wouldn't you be angry if you lost half your face and looked like a monster?"

Finally. Ha! There it was.

"Oh, Kelley, you don't look like a monster," Leah said calmly.

"Yeah, *sure.* You're just saying that because you're my sister. There isn't a kid at my school who wouldn't look at me right now and *freak out!*"

"That's not true," Leah argued. "They know what happened. You're not giving them a chance—"

"No! Nothing else matters! *Looks* matter. Trust me, I know. You look weird, you wear the wrong shoes—the wrong kind of pants, you are *out*. You don't get a second chance!"

"But the kids at your school already know who you are. They know there's more to Kelley Brennan than just her face—"

"There is no more Kelley Brennan! Not the Kelley they knew! She's gone. There's just a stupid mask here! Don't you understand? That's all they're going to see!"

"Kelley, you're making this so difficult for yourself."

Kelley shook her head. "You don't understand, Leah, because everything is so easy for you."

"But it's not as bad as you think—"

"Not as bad as I think?!" She repeated loudly, staring at Leah. "How can you say that? I have been through absolute hell! No one in this world will ever begin to know what I went through!"

"I didn't mean to say you didn't suffer—"

Kelley cut her off. "I almost died!"

"Yes, I know, but—"

"That engine smacked into my face!"

"Kelley—"

"Hot metal, Leah! They had to *pry* a melted earring out of my flesh!"

Leah put a hand over her mouth.

"The skin on my leg?! Ha! You should have seen it, Leah! Third-degree burn, they call it! That leg looked like a piece of burned meat!"

Tears sprang up in Leah's eyes. She reached out and tried to touch Kelley's hand. "But you lived, Kelley. Thank God you lived."

Kelley yanked her hand away and picked at the edge of the Jobst glove. She knew she was being unreasonable—and *mean* again, too. But she couldn't stop herself—because even her sister couldn't understand!

"You're so smart, Leah. Why do you think I was chosen to be in an accident? Huh? Aunt Katherine says everything happens for a reason. What reason did God have for choosing me? What *lesson* was I supposed to learn?"

Leah pressed her fingertips together and took a deep breath.

"First of all," she began slowly, "you're assuming that I agree with Aunt Katherine. Which I don't. I don't believe everything happens for a reason."

Kelley's eyebrow went up. "Oh? You don't believe in God now?"

"Wait a minute!" She threw open her hands. "Who said I didn't believe in God? I said I didn't believe that everything happens for a reason. It's *not* the same thing."

Kelley was skeptical. She crossed her arms and narrowed her eyes.

Leah continued. "I don't think your accident was preordained by a superior being—or destined to happen from the minute you were born. I don't think God is a . . . a *micromanager* that way! I mean, sometimes, Kelley, there is no one—or nothing—to blame."

*No one to blame.* The phrase ricocheted in Kelley's head.

"By the way," Leah said. "You're wrong about me. Everything is not easy for me. Obviously, this isn't. So maybe I'm not so smart after all."

Leah paused. "But I do know this, Kelley. You are twelve years old and you have a long life in front of you. You can choose to make it a happy life. Or you can choose to make it a sad life. The choice is yours."

Kelley remained silent.

Leah didn't press anymore. "I don't know what else to say," she said, sounding defeated.

Isn't that what Kelley wanted?

"I guess we'll call it a day." Leah dropped her hands into her lap and then stood, gathering up the books.

She hesitated, as though not knowing what she should do, then set the books back down on the coffee table and touched Kelley's shoulder. "Give yourself a chance," she said, before leaving the room.

# seventeen

AFTER LEAH LEFT FOR WORK that afternoon, Kelley sat at the kitchen table, lost in thought. She didn't even move when Tigger rubbed up against the back of her leg. Eventually she noticed a note her mother had left for her under the pepper shaker: *Kelley—There's a fruit salad for you in the fridge.*

She went to the refrigerator to get a Coke and saw the beautiful plate her mother had fixed: strawberries, grapes, melon balls, and slices of date bread spread with cream cheese surrounding a big scoop of cottage cheese. She knew it had taken time and effort to fix a lunch like that.

But Kelley wasn't hungry. She took the Coke with one hand and one of her crutches with the other and limped into the living room to make a telephone call. She found the number for the nurses' station at the burn unit, kicked off her shoes, and tapped in the numbers. An unfamiliar voice answered.

"Hi," Kelley said timidly. "My name's Kelley Brennan. Could I speak to Leslie, please?"

Sorry, she was told, but Leslie was with a patient. Was there someone else who could help her?

"No," Kelley said. "I need to talk to Leslie."

Sorry, the receptionist said again, but what was Kelley's last name? Was she a family member of a patient?

"I *was* a patient!" Kelley replied angrily.

Oh. Would she like the number for the outpatient burn clinic then?

"No!" Kelley exclaimed. "I *have* it. I need to talk to Leslie. Can she please call me back?"

She knew Leslie would call the minute she saw Kelley's name on the slip of paper. After all, they hadn't talked once since Kelley had returned home. She popped open the Coke and sat, waiting.

She hadn't thought exactly what she would say. *Leslie, hi. It's me, Kelley. I just thought I'd call. Did you know? My sister's here.* Then Leslie would ask how Kelley was doing, if anything was bothering her. *As a matter of fact,* Kelley might say, *I never asked you this before. But do you think people get burned for a reason? I mean, you've seen a lot of people like me. Have you ever made sense of it?*

Kelley picked up the remote and flipped through the channels on television. A half hour passed. There was nothing to watch but soaps and pathetic talk shows and

Kelley did not want to listen to someone else's problems. Retrieving her lunch from the refrigerator, she sat on the couch, eating the strawberries one by one. When she finished, she ate the grapes. Then, finally, the date bread.

Her schoolbooks were on the coffee table. The pictures of the least terns were on top of the pile. Kelley ignored them and picked up last night's newspaper, which was folded open to the page with all the movies. Her mother and Leah had circled a couple, but Kelley would say no. She was not about to take the chance of going to the mall.

She looked at the phone and waited. Apparently, Leslie was not going to call back right away.

Kelley set down her lunch and picked up the photographs. They were black-and-white pictures. Simple, boring pictures of gray birds and gravel. Little nests and tiny eggs. It was probably true that most people in this world couldn't care less about these birds. But was it really true that if they disappeared it wouldn't matter?

There was a slight twinge deep inside. Kelley's eyes glazed over.

Strange, Kelley thought, but sometimes she felt as though she lived in a series of boxes. The biggest box was Kelley on the outside. This was the Kelley who was burned and mean, who wore a mask and was angry at the world for what had happened.

A medium-size box contained the halfway Kelley, the obedient, placid Kelley who did her hand and mouth and leg exercises faithfully, who wore her Jobst and her plastic mask, who ate her meals on time, and went to bed at ten.

Finally, way down deep, there was a tiny little box that contained Kelley on the inside. This was basically the same old Kelley who had always been there, just kind of shrunk and beaten down.

Big boxes, little boxes. Weak versus strong, and strong was wrong, she was thinking.

Stupid birds.

*"It's just a little bird . . . I held one in the palm of my hand last year . . . We in Maryland should care . . ."*

She said that the day of the accident. The day she got up early to paint the world on her left thumbnail. The day the sixth grade planted a dogwood tree in recognition of Earth Day. Alison and Liesel sat before her in the front row. Daniel stood watching with a secret gift in his hand . . . Kelley took a deep breath and spoke into the portable microphone. *"This little bird has a right to live . . ."*

Kelley stared at the pictures, then slumped back in the couch, confused, and let the photographs fall from her lap.

# eighteen

"THERE IS A TURNING POINT," Dr. Brewer was telling a group of visiting medical students, "when you know whether a burn patient is going to live or not. Of course, an infection can always set in during the weeks following a serious burn, but if the patient has lost the will, the desire to the live—if that spirit is gone, there is not much modern medicine can do."

He paused outside the small examining room, where Kelley waited with her mother, and one of the students asked Dr. Brewer a question. It had been a week since Kelley was released from the hospital, and this was her first visit back. Now she leaned forward in her chair so she could hear through the small crack in the door, but Dr. Brewer's soft, accented voice was already growing dimmer and soon was lost as he moved off down the hall, followed by his white-coated entourage.

His words left Kelley hanging, wondering what her turning point had been. What was it Dr. Brewer had seen in her?

Odd, but now that she looked back, she could not remember thinking that she ever wanted to just give up. Sure, there were times when the pain was so great she wished she weren't alive. Times when she screamed that she wanted to die. But somehow, it wasn't the same thing. Not really. That was just anger. Underneath it, even in the deepest, darkest hospital days, there had always been a forward line of thinking. *Just get through this . . . In twenty minutes the medicine will kick in . . . Mom will be here at seven . . .*

Restless, Kelley took off the Jobst glove, then her mask, and set them both on the examining table beside her. Her mother glanced at her over the magazine she was reading. "You okay?"

"Just getting ready," Kelley said.

She had been anxious about returning for the burn clinic, but so far, the morning had been uneventful. The burn clinic was on a different floor from the burn unit, for one thing. And for another, Kelley didn't feel alone.

Sitting in the waiting room, which they did for almost an hour, Kelley was surrounded by others who had been burned. There was an older woman whose entire forearm was one big, bumpy red scar, and beside her a fidgety young man in blue jeans and a white T-shirt who talked quite openly about being burned on both legs by acid at a factory in Dundalk where he worked. He cracked jokes about his Jobst stockings. He said now he understood how uncomfortable a ballet dancer must feel. "Must be why they can jump so high!" he chortled.

Kelley thought he was pretty stupid, but a woman sitting across from him laughed at almost everything he said. She wore a neck brace and talked a blue streak, so everyone in the room knew she had suffered a second-degree steam burn at the restaurant where she worked in Essex.

Kelley kept her eyes averted and no one spoke to her. She had brought a book but couldn't get interested. Idly, she picked up a brochure on burn prevention from the end table beside her and scanned it:

> *Fire is the fourth greatest cause of accidental death in the United States. It is surpassed only by motor vehicle accidents, falls, and drowning as a cause of unintentional injury death. Each year, an estimated 20,000 adults and children die, and an additional 75,000 to 100,000 are hospitalized, from fire-related injuries.*

She was one in 100,000. Now there was a pathetic thought. Imagine, all those people—all that pain. She didn't want to read about the million ways that it could happen and how to prevent it. She did not care. It had happened to her. With a limp hand, she dropped the brochure back on the table.

"Would you like to go out for lunch afterward?" her mother asked, closing up her magazine.

"I thought you had to get back to work," Kelley said.

"I can take time for lunch," her mother said, sounding a little hurt.

Kelley didn't mean to make her feel bad. Did she?

"Maybe," Kelley said, disturbed that these conflicting feelings still haunted her.

Her mother smiled hopefully. "We'll see how you feel."

At last, a nurse named Carol called Kelley's name and ushered them into a small examining room. Carol took Kelley's temperature and blood pressure, then helped her up onto the scale, which showed that she had gained three pounds since being home.

"Are you having any problems?" Carol asked.

The question struck Kelley as funny. She hesitated. Was she having any problems? She looked at Carol, and Carol must have seen something in that look, because she put her hand on Kelley's arm and rephrased it. "I know this must be terribly hard. A lot of adjustment for you. But is there anything that's hurting, that doesn't feel as though it's healing properly?"

Kelley thought. "The only thing," she said, "is that my leg itches, where the pins came out. And sometimes, when I open my mouth, it hurts a little here." She pointed to the right-hand corner of her mouth.

When Dr. Brewer finally came in to check, he paid special attention to the corner of Kelley's mouth. He said there appeared to be some contracture on her face, where the skin was healing too tightly. "It may soften and lengthen with time," he said. "We'll have to wait and see."

"What if it doesn't?" Kelley asked.

"Then we may have to do some surgery. There are skin tension lines on everyone's face," he explained. "Sometimes what we have to do is recut scars so they blend in better with these natural lines. If you let it go, the contracture might pull your mouth down, so it looked as though you were always frowning. You wouldn't want that, would you?"

Kelley shook her head.

Next, Dr. Brewer lightly pressed his index finger over Kelley's right eye and reminded her how Dr. LaMotte, the plastic surgeon, would take a slice of skin from her scalp and fashion an eyebrow for her. Probably in another year, he said, after the skin had completely healed.

He lifted Kelley's hands and turned them over. "Are you still drawing?" he asked with a smile.

It pleased Kelley that he remembered. "Yes," she said.

The leg was last. Now that the new grafted skin on her leg was healing, it was time for a Jobst stocking, to prevent the puffy, hypertrophic scarring. "Carol will show you how to wear it," Dr. Brewer said, making some notes on his clipboard. "We'll see you back here next week, okay?"

The nurse gave Kelley and her mother two sets of Jobst stockings, then helped Kelley put one of the brown knit stockings on. It was like thick panty hose, except that it had only one leg.

Carol also handed her a small card with a name and

phone number printed on it. "This woman can help you if you're feeling sad and want to talk about things," she said. She looked over Kelley's head to her mother. "Sometimes other family members benefit from the counseling, too.

"And here's a pamphlet about a summer camp in West Virginia for children who have been burned. It's all kids, some of them your age, who are working through the same things," she explained to Kelley. "Think about it, why don't you?"

Kelley thanked her, and took the card and the pamphlet to be polite.

"I just want to go home," Kelley said as they made their way out of the hospital after physical therapy.

She heard her mother sigh.

"Is there some tuna?" Kelley asked, adjusting the crutches under her arms. "We could make tuna fish sandwiches and sit out back."

"All right. But I do have to stop and get some mayonnaise."

Kelley flashed her a look.

"Don't worry," her mother said. "You can wait in the car."

Kelley buckled her seat belt and turned to look out the window. She wriggled uncomfortably, aware of the snug, new Jobst. Inside, she grew even tighter. She did not want to go back to the hospital and have more surgery.

She could feel the anger pulling her down again. Bad luck. Bad timing. A red light. A speeding truck. Quentin Hall. Kelley couldn't hate him, could she?

"Whatever happened to that truck driver?" she blurted out.

"Why?" The question startled her mother. "Why are you asking about *him?*"

"I just wondered what happened, that's all."

"They said he had a concussion. And broke his collarbone. Something about his vision? I'm surprised you'd want to know," her mother said.

Kelley let the subject drop.

"So tell me how the tutoring is going," her mother said.

Kelley shrugged. "Okay, I guess."

Here it was—an opportunity to talk with her mother the way they used to talk—and it was being ruined. Ruined because Kelley on the outside was elbowing her selfish way up front to slam the door shut and punish her mother.

Nervously, Kelley pinched at the edge of her mask.


Soon after they crossed the bridge to Kent Island, Kelley's mother pulled into the parking lot of a large shopping center. "I'll leave the engine running so you can have the air-conditioning," she said.

It felt a little scary to be sitting in a car in a crowded parking lot because at any moment someone could walk by and see her. Kelley kept her face turned in and listened to the music. By and by, however, she snuck a look, and when several minutes had passed and still no one came close, she grew more courageous and sat up, looking straight out the front windshield.

From here, she realized, she could see the Islander Hardware Store. She turned off the music, moved by the memory of that day last year when she had walked by that store and something on the sidewalk had caught her eye. It had looked like a little ball of fluff with legs. Cornered behind a trash can, it grew still and had allowed Kelley to take it in her hands.

"A baby bird," she'd murmured, moved by the extraordinary find. Cupping it gently in her hands, she went into the hardware store.

"Excuse me," she'd said to a clerk. "I found this baby bird outside on the sidewalk."

The man had barely looked at her. He was putting price tags on wooden rake handles. "Darn things," he grumbled. "They nest up on the roof. Dozens of 'em every year. Half them little ones end up in the parking lot."

"They do?" Kelley asked incredulously.

"I told those people with the state if they wanted to do something, go ahead. They're some kind of endangered bird or something. But, man, I don't have time to go saving no wildlife around here."

The bird's tiny feet felt like toothpicks against her palm. When she peeked in through the small hole between her thumb and forefinger, she saw a miniature face with eyes like delicate beads.

"What should I do?" Kelley asked the man.

"Beats me." He shrugged. "Humane Society, maybe. It won't live, though."

At home, Kelley put the bird in an empty hamster cage. She made one telephone call after another until she found a woman at the Maryland Department of Natural Resources who told her the bird was probably a baby least tern that had fallen off the roof.

"It's a threatened species in Maryland," she said. "We really ought to get the tern back to its nest as soon as possible."

She agreed to meet Kelley the next morning in front of the hardware store. She said if she had to, she'd get a fire truck to get that one little bird back up on the roof. Kelley was excited.

"What can I give it to eat?" she asked. "Some bird seed?"

The woman laughed. "No. Nothing like that. At this age the little ones need their parents to bring them small fish and aquatic stuff. Just give it some water and keep it warm and quiet."

Kelley put a towel over the cage and set it on the floor by her bed. She even closed her door so Tigger wouldn't come in and scare it during the night. But by morning, the little tern had died.

"This never should have happened," Kelley had said in her Earth Day speech nine months later. "The least terns nest on the roof because they have lost the beaches where they used to live. We took those beaches for our marinas and our parks and our waterfront homes. The least terns are as much a part of this world as we are. They have a right to be here. It is time for us to help." Mrs. Fox hugged her. Daniel gave her a thumbs-up.

Sitting in the car, Kelley stared up at the roof of the hardware store and could see the top of the chicken-wire fence. Leaning forward, she could see them now—terns, dozens of them, wheeling above the roof. Tears came to her eyes. She smiled, pleased to think that her fence had stopped the babies from falling off the roof into the parking lot.

Kelley felt the tears running under her mask. A rare wave of happiness rippled through her. Maybe she could draw this very scene to complete the science project. Mr. Canone would like that—integrating art with science! The idea excited her, made her itchy for a pad of paper and a drawing pencil.

Then, suddenly, something else in the parking lot caught her attention. Two people walking toward a car—and one of them was Alison!

What was she doing here? Kelley wondered. Why was she back from North Carolina so early? Were the twins too much for her? She wouldn't blame her if she had quit. Of course, Kelley thought, if she had read Alison's last couple of letters she might have known.

Heat, bouncing off the hot black asphalt made things shimmer. Kelley squinted, trying to see Alison better. She had her hair pulled back, but it seemed shorter—much shorter. Had she cut it? Her beautiful long dark hair?

The woman and Alison stopped at a blue sedan. Kelley thought about opening her window and calling out to her. *Alison! Over here! It's me, Kelley! Look at the terns! There must be hundreds of them!* She knew Alison would rush over. All that stuff since the accident would be forgotten, including that day in the hospital when Kelley said something out of anger. She couldn't even remember what it was now! *I didn't mean to hurt you, Alison. Really, you should have come back again. I wanted you to come back.*

They finished loading their bags into the trunk of the car, and now the woman was opening the car with her key. Alison stood waiting on the passenger's side. Kelley's finger pressed the button that opened the window.

*A face first, then a mask.* She didn't want to scare them. Alison had never seen the mask, but she would understand. She needed Alison to see her. *Oh, Alison, please turn and look at me. I miss you!*

The window went down, and heat flowed into the car.

The girl turned.

And Kelley could see that it wasn't Alison after all.

# nineteen

THE NEXT DAY, WHEN THE math paper still hadn't been done, Leah guessed at Kelley's secret plan.

"You don't want to do the work because you don't want to go back to school," she said. "Do you?"

It caught Kelley off guard. She had been sitting on a straight-back chair in the living room, lifting her right leg up and slowly letting it down on the count of five, but now she stopped to look at Leah.

Leah had her running clothes on, her hair up in a ponytail, and sat, drumming her fingers on the ends of an armchair. "I did a lot of thinking about this yesterday while you were gone, Kelley."

"You did?"

She crossed her arms and looked very serious. "I understand how you feel, Kelley. But I am *not* going to waste my time with someone who won't cooperate. So here's my proposal. If you do the work and still don't want to go back to school at the end of summer, I will convince Mom that you need to do a year at home."

"Do you mean it?" Kelley asked.

"Cross my heart. I'll research the home-school programs, everything."

Leah stood and threw up her hands. "That's it! It'll be a deal, between you and me. Mom doesn't even have to know. Agreed?"

Kelley still suspected there was more to this deal than Leah was saying. A bit uncertainly, she nodded. "Agreed."

The following morning was overcast and cooler, so Leah suggested they go outside on the deck. Kelley sat with her baseball cap on beneath the patio umbrella.

"One minute before we start," Leah said, stepping back to shake out a small white tablecloth. She draped the material over a card table and then set down a blue enameled pitcher filled with bright orange zinnias.

Kelley shifted the books on her lap and stared quizzically at the arrangement.

Beside the pitcher, Leah placed a shiny dark eggplant. "For your drawing lesson," she finally explained. "As soon as we get the biology and the math done."

"My drawing lesson?"

"Yup. I reread my notes from art class last night. This is

called a still life." Leah gathered up her long hair and secured it with a huge gold clip. "Have you ever done one?"

Kelley shook her head.

"I haven't either!" Leah laughed. "But we did attempt one in class. Mine was so horrible I never even finished it."

She took a seat opposite Kelley and tapped on the science book. "Let's see what you remember first. An amethyst crystal. Organic or inorganic?"

Kelley knew instantly because she had read the chapter last night. "Inorganic," she said.

"A mushroom?"

"Organic." It was part of the deal after all.

"Table salt?"

"Inorganic." It didn't make any sense to hold back, Kelley had decided. She would end up doing the work anyway. Why not now?

"Aluminum?"

"Inorganic."

Their eyes met. "Great!" Leah exclaimed.

Kelley blushed.

She had done the math, too. When they got to it an hour later, Kelley pulled out the completed assignments and the calculator from the side pocket of her backpack. While she waited for Leah, she adjusted the waistband of the Jobst stocking—she still wasn't used to it—and studied the still life. "Remember those pastels you sent me while I was in the hospital? Maybe I should get them," she said.

Leah held up a finger. "Uh-uh. Not yet. After the math."

Finally, when it was time for the art lesson, Leah said Kelley would have to do a warm-up exercise first.

"Oh, come on," Kelley moaned.

"No, no. You'll like this! It's called a blind profile. I'm going to sit sideways, looking off toward the water, and you're going to draw my contour, the outside lines of what you see—*without looking* at your paper."

"Without looking?"

"The point is to focus on what you see," Leah explained.

Kelley positioned the pencil and studied Leah's profile.

"Go slow," her sister said, trying not to move her lips much. "Imagine there are pencils coming out of your eyes."

Forehead . . . nose . . . lips . . . Kelley tried to feel each of them as she drew. When she was finished, she and Leah looked at it together and chuckled, because the drawing was so terribly out of proportion.

"Try again," Leah said. She struck the same pose, but Kelley hesitated because a bizarre thought had emerged: If she were in Leah's position, sitting sideways with someone drawing her profile from the left, her face would appear perfectly normal. From the left—from one side—Kelley realized, no one would ever know she'd been burned. Sitting in a theater or on a bus, standing in line at the grocery store or at the amusement park . . .

"How are we doing?" Leah asked.

"Okay," Kelley said, staring at the paper.

She could not let the thought bog her down.

She moved the pencil.

No one went through life as a profile.

"Good," Leah said. "Much better."

She handed a pad of gray pastel paper to Kelley. "Now. Have you ever worked with charcoal?"

"No."

Leah gave her three sticks of charcoal and a small eraser.

"What's this for? In case I make a mistake?"

"Exactly. It's a special eraser for charcoal and pastels that picks up the residue."

Kelley was intrigued. She made a few marks with one of the charcoal sticks, and Leah smudged one of them with her finger so Kelley could see the effect.

"Neat," Kelley said. "What should I draw?"

"The still life," Leah said, pointing toward the table. "When you do the eggplant, though, I want you to draw its shadow, too. This is called a cast shadow. It'll give that eggplant some weight. Make it *sit* on that table." She leaned close and whispered to Kelley, "Are you impressed with the notes I took?"

Kelley smiled up at her.

But Leah was checking her watch. "Yikes, I need to get going! I have a dentist appointment before work. Keep going, though. Don't be afraid to smudge the charcoal with your fingers. Like that, yes! And remember the shadowing. Make it *sit* there."

Kelley worked on the flowers and the eggplant long after Leah had left. She was pleased with the result. Her eggplant was fat and shiny and, with its shadow, did seem to have weight to it. It even started to look appetizing, she thought. Maybe because she had never eaten lunch! She leaned back in her chair and admired her eggplant once more.

As she did, a warm breeze made its way up to the deck, carrying with it the faint, earthy smell of marsh at low tide. Kelley watched a pair of mallards fly in, scudding across the water like little water-skiers, while in the shallows, not far away, a great blue heron stalked an afternoon snack.

Kelley flipped to a clean sheet of pastel paper and began sketching the long-legged heron. In his beak, she drew a fish with a floppy tail. The heron stood in the water, which she extended across the page, smudging it with her finger, to where she drew in wispy sea grass and dark, heavy-headed cattails.

She paused to look critically at what she had done, and a bold thought occurred to her. But why not? she wondered. New doors opened for other people all the time. Maybe this is how it happened. A door closes, another one opens. Maybe she *could* take art lessons. Not now, but in a couple years. And just say she was good enough that the art lessons led to art school. She could illustrate greeting cards or children's books—or become a movie animator! *Wow.*

She gazed back at the water and noticed how the sunlight, reflecting off the wind-driven ripples near shore, seemed to be rushing toward her.

Two more weeks went by. Kelley did her schoolwork every day and soon was caught up in math and history. Her leg was stronger. She even started to play the piano again. Short, simple pieces that didn't tire her right hand too much. She was finishing a song called "Ancient Temple" one afternoon when the telephone rang.

Kelley got up to answer it and was inside the door to her mother's office before remembering she didn't touch the phone. Never. Not even the day her father phoned from Montreal: "I think I've got a new job lined up, and I'll try to get down to see you girls in September." Or the afternoon Antonio, in his Italian accent, left a message for Leah. Nor *both* times Leslie called back to say "hi."

The phone rang once more before the answering machine kicked in. Kelley froze upon hearing Daniel's voice.

"Sorry I haven't been in touch," he said. "I've been working for my dad at the marina this summer. I can't wait for school to start so I can have a vacation!" He laughed a little, nervously, and said that he hoped she was doing okay. And, oh, there was one other reason he was calling.

"I'm going up on the roof again next week," he said. "Mr. Banker got me permission. I want to get some pictures before the terns take off. They're going to migrate soon. Early August, he said. You ought to see them, Kelley. They're really something. I've got a new lens I want to try out and I would love to get one of those birds flying right at me. That little white spot on their head? Remember how it looked just like a headlight coming at you?"

There was a pause. Kelley sat at her mother's desk and rested her hands on the ink blotter, just inches from the telephone and Daniel's voice.

"Anyway, I was hoping you could be there. I'm going to give Eric and Melissa a call. I think Melissa's in Ocean City, though." A slight pause. "If you can make it, please come. We're going up next Saturday at nine. I'll hope to see you. Take care." A quick click. He was gone.

Kelley pushed the "repeat" button to hear the message again. Three times she did this. Of course, there was no way she'd go up on the roof with them. It was out of the question. Daniel had never even seen her since the accident. He was part of another world. Still, it was nice that he had called. She listened one last time to the message, savoring each word—*I'll hope to see you*—before erasing it so her mother would never know.

# twenty

"I THINK MY FAVORITE IS the pencil sketch of Alison. The expression on her face, the long, sleek hair flowing over her shoulder. It's *wonderful,*" Leah was saying. She had the car for the day and was driving Kelley to Baltimore for her appointment with Dr. LaMotte.

Their mother had a ride to work and was already in an important meeting in Annapolis. She tried to explain to the girls before she left that a home-equity loan was something people obtained when they didn't want to use their savings: "It's just to tide us over," she said. But Leah was quiet, and Kelley was not naive; she knew this meant they needed the money.

"And the eyes—Kelley, you are so good with eyes!" Leah went on.

"Thanks," Kelley said shyly. The sketch *was* good. She had drawn Alison by looking at a photograph her friend sent. *What do you think, Kel? Double holes in my right ear! Can you see 'em?*

One night, in a feverish change of mind, Kelley had ripped open and read through all of Alison's and Liesel's latest letters. *I want to be your friend, Kelley. You need to tell me how*, Alison implored. And Liesel so generous: *If you want any more of my CDs, tell my mom.* Even Alison's dumb jokes made her feel warm inside: *How do you communicate with a fish? You drop him a line!*

"Antonio was asking about you when he called last night," Leah continued. "I was telling him about the drawing. I told him that the greatest thing about it was that you weren't drawing to please anyone or to *emulate your wonderful sister, Leah*. It's all *you!* It's all Kelley!"

Embarrassed, but flattered, Kelley looked away shyly and readjusted the sweater on her lap.

"You remind me when we get home," Leah said. "I picked up that schedule of art classes. Registration for fall starts next week."

Kelley smoothed a wrinkle in her long skirt. Leah was forgetting that Kelley was not going back to school in September. So why would she want to sign up for art classes now?


In the waiting room at Dr. LaMotte's office, Kelley took a seat and pulled out a small paperback book from her purse to read. Leah selected a magazine and sat beside her. The room was not very crowded. Kelley's eyes swept over the other patients, but did a double take when she spotted a young girl, about her own age, sitting across from her. She was reading the exact same book as Kelley: *Where the Red Fern Grows,* by Wilson Rawls. Amazing. She looked up at the girl's face and their eyes met.

"We must have the same summer reading list," the girl said brightly.

Amused, Kelley nodded. "Yeah, we must."

"How far are you?"

Kelley glanced down at the page she was on. "I just started Chapter Four."

The girl nodded. "I'm almost done." She had short red hair the color of Liesel's and a black string choker like one Kelley owned. "It's a really good book," she said. "You'll like it."

"I think so," Kelley replied. Suddenly feeling self-conscious, and not knowing what else to say, she turned her attention back to the book.

A woman crossed the room. "Christine, we can go now," she said, and the girl got up to leave.

Kelley was disappointed, but she knew the girl would look back one more time. She did. She turned to Kelley and smiled. "Good luck," she said.

Kelley lifted her hand slightly to wave. "Thanks."

She went back to her book again, but the words floated in front of her. She wondered why the girl was here. She didn't look as though she needed a plastic surgeon. Maybe she was here with her mother because her mother was the patient. That was probably it. Lucky her. She was nice, though. Christine. At least Christine was nice, Kelley thought.

Kelley's name was called then.

"Do you want me to go with you?" Leah asked.

"It's okay," Kelley said.

In Dr. LaMotte's office, she took off her mask and the surgeon examined her face carefully, lifting her chin and looking at her from all angles. "It's healing beautifully," he said. "Although I think we are going to have to do something right here, on the corner of your mouth, probably before school starts.

"Is everything else okay, Kelley? Do you have any questions?" Dr. LaMotte asked.

Kelley gathered up her sweater and her purse and hesitated with the mask in her hands.

"Actually, I do," Kelley said. She looked up at Dr. LaMotte. "I wondered, in a year or so when you're finished doing everything, what I'll look like. I mean I know I won't look beautiful or anything, but . . . well, what exactly *will* I look like?"

Dr. LaMotte listened patiently and waited for her to finish. There was great compassion in his eyes. "You know Dr. Brewer and I have always been frank," he began.

Kelley felt her heart drop.

"We have told you before that you won't look *exactly* the way you used to, Kelley. You have to accept that. Hey—look at me—you are going to be okay. The skin on the right side of your face will have a little different color to it. But this is where makeup comes in. Someone on the staff will show you how to use cosmetics to even the skin tone out and make you look more natural.

"But even then," he warned, "you have to remember that the whole point of makeup is to make yourself look natural, and natural is not perfect."

He paused a moment and got up to pull a large black spiral notebook from off a bookshelf in the room. He flipped it open.

"Have you ever seen this picture?" he asked, setting the opened book down on the examining table beside Kelley.

Kelley nodded. She recognized the picture instantly as one she had seen on a poster in the hospital urging donations to the local burn unit. It was the photograph of a human face so blackened by a burn that it was impossible to tell even if the face belonged to a man or a woman.

Total third degree, Kelley was sure. This was a burn so devastating it had destroyed almost all of the facial features this person once had: eyebrows, eyelashes, lips—even an ear. Kelley shivered with an uncanny knowledge of the pain and suffering this poster represented. She wondered if this person had lived and couldn't help but think that, in this case, it would have been a blessing to have died.

Dr. LaMotte turned the page to show her the picture of an ordinary, but pleasant-looking woman with thick, dark, curly hair and wire-rimmed glasses.

"Same woman, three years later," he said.

Kelley's mouth dropped. She looked at Dr. LaMotte

and then back at the photograph in disbelief. She returned to the previous page, then flipped it forward again. "But this woman on the poster lost her ear."

"So we made a new one—from one of her ribs," Dr. LaMotte said.

Kelley restudied the photograph.

"I had another patient in here just before you," Dr. LaMotte went on. "A girl about your same age, I would guess."

"Christine?" Kelley ventured.

"Yes. Do you know her?"

Kelley shook her head. "No, but I saw her in the waiting room. We were reading the same book."

Dr. LaMotte grinned.

"Christine was burned?"

"I work for the burn unit," Dr. LaMotte reminded her.

"But she looked perfect!"

Dr. LaMotte raised his eyebrows. "Nobody's perfect, Kelley."

"What happened to her?"

"She was in a house fire, almost a year ago now. She tried to open a window, but the frame was burning. She had a lot of third degree on her hands, under her chin," Dr. LaMotte said. "I did a pretty big graft up along her neck. And you probably didn't notice, but there are no fingers on Christine's left hand. We had to take them off after the fire, and graft skin onto the fingers of her right hand, and the palms of both hands."

Kelley sighed in sympathy and stared down at her own

hands, at the one in the brown Jobst that was going to draw her a future. God, she thought, at least she had her hands.

"The best surgeon in the world couldn't give Christine a new set of fingers, Kelley. But let me tell you something, that kid is a trooper. The clarinet had to go, but other than that, she does most everything she did before. She is still a straight-A student—she's still on the swim team!"

Dr. LaMotte put a hand on Kelley's knee and looked into her eyes. "Christine did not let her loss change who she was."

Slowly, Kelley lifted her mask. Dr. LaMotte helped her to refasten it.

A rib for an ear, she was thinking. A hand that would never sift beach sand, wear a ring, braid hair, or throw a Frisbee.

In this world, Kelley realized, she was not alone.

# twenty-one

KELLEY WAS GRATEFUL THAT LEAH didn't ask any questions as they left the hospital. They walked back to the car in silence.

The day had started out cloudy; now it was drizzling. Familiar landmarks flashed by and scenery melded together as they proceeded down the interstate. It wasn't until Leah was onto Light Street, near the baseball stadium, that Kelley realized they weren't headed home after all.

"Where are you going?"

"A little surprise," Leah said, flicking the windshield wipers on. "I told Mom I wanted to take you to an art gallery."

"An art gallery?"

"Yeah. See some good examples of art. Goodness knows I can't do anything more for you."

Kelley's lips made a tight line as she turned to look out her window. The windshield wipers thumped noisily.

"Look," Leah said, "I'll take you home right now if you want. Just say the word and I'll turn around. But I'm asking you, Kelley, to give it a try. You *need* to do this."

Kelley would not look at her.

"Have you ever heard of the Walters Art Gallery?"

Kelley didn't answer; she felt as though she'd been tricked.

"It's nice," Leah said. "And it's not huge. I thought we could poke around a little, then have something to eat. There's a nice café there."

Kelley kept her gaze out the window. She did not feel like fighting.

"Come on, Kelley. Relax. Let yourself enjoy this."

Sure, Kelley thought, *enjoy.*

Charles Street in Baltimore was busy at midday, but they found a place to park close to the gallery. Leah fed several quarters into the meter, then fished the crutches out of the backseat in case Kelley got tired and needed them later on.

Kelley was glad for the rain. It meant that most people would be scurrying along and might not notice her. Still, she kept her head down and made her way as quickly as she could up the sidewalk as Leah strode beside her, holding an umbrella for them both.

Inside the lobby, Kelley backed up against a wall, where she waited while Leah paid for their tickets. Air-conditioning made the lobby chilly. Kelley put her sweater on and readjusted the long, thin handle of her purse over her shoulder. There weren't many people, she noticed. She was relieved.

Leah returned with a map and an orange sticker for Kelley to press onto her clothing.

"Let's go see the Impressionists first," Leah said as they rode the elevator to the fourth floor. "I *love* the Impressionists. Someday, Kelley, I want to take you to this little museum in Paris. I forget the name—it's near Place de la Concorde. But it's full of Monet's huge water lilies. They're gigantic—room-size! I mean, you walk in and you feel as though you're in this beautiful, heavenly garden. It is so incredible."

The elevator doors opened. Kelley was relieved again that so few people were here. In fact, there was only one elderly couple that she could see.

"Look," Leah whispered, "there's a Monet—and a Degas. Oh, this'll be great. Come here, I want to show you something."

Kelley let Leah guide her attention toward a painting called *The Church at Éragny* by Camille Pissarro. It was a restful, pleasing picture, Kelley thought. A church, a fence, some grass and trees on a cloudy day.

"Now come close," Leah said, "and *look* at this painting."

Kelley stepped up close until she was practically nose to nose with the work of art.

"See how, when you're close up, it becomes fragmented," Leah said. "You can see the brush strokes and the unusual colors you would normally never think of using: the purple in the trees, the green on the roof. And look, the bright emerald spot here, in the leaves. Close up, it's almost unrecognizable."

She was right. Kelley was fascinated.

"One of my art teachers made us do this in Paris, and it just bowled me over. What she was trying to show us, though, is that the Impressionists strived to capture a moment in time by painting quickly and using the effects of light on objects."

Kelley nodded. She could see it.

"Now back up," Leah told her.

Kelley retraced her steps, then turned and studied the Pissarro again. Interesting how, from afar, the picture as a whole was so different—and so beautiful. She couldn't see the purple in the trees now, or that spot of emerald. It all blended in.

If only people in the future would do that for her, Kelley couldn't help but think. Step back and see her for who she was—instead of focusing on the harsh brush strokes of her scars. Leslie's voice from far away echoed in her head: *You have to learn to be good at second impressions, Kel.*


Kelley didn't balk at the suggestion to eat lunch. She was tired and hungry by the time they had finished with the fourth floor.

"May I suggest *la salade du jardin,*" Leah said with her best French accent. She leaned over the marble tabletop in the museum's small café and handed Kelley a menu. "It's made with hydroponic greens."

Kelley grinned and pulled the napkin into her lap. She

was still nervous, being in a public place like this. Quickly, she scanned the menu and ordered a salad and crab cakes. Leah ordered pasta—and blueberry soup for two.

When the soup arrived, Kelley quietly removed her mask and set it on the chair beside her. She didn't think anyone was watching, but she didn't have the heart to look around and see.

Kelley had never had blueberry soup. It was cool and sweet.

"I wanted to ask you something," Leah said, folding her hands on the table. She looked so pretty, so sophisticated, Kelley thought, with her long hair pulled into a French twist, the bright pink lipstick.

"Go ahead," Kelley said.

"Are you still thinking you won't go to school this year?"

Kelley paused, with her hand on the soup spoon. The truth was that she was having second thoughts. "I'm afraid it'll be really lonely," she said.

She glanced at Leah and saw that her sister was waiting for her to go on. "Maybe I should talk to Liesel and Alison when they get back. See what they think."

Leah's eyebrows went up.

Kelley looked at her sadly. "I miss them," she said.

"I know you do," Leah replied. She reached over to touch Kelley's hand and hesitated a moment. "If it helps you any, you should know that Alison and Liesel—and all the kids in your class—understand about your face, and the need for the mask."

"What do you mean?"

"Well, I wasn't sure I should tell you this, but a nurse from the burn unit came down in June before school ended. Her name was Leslie. I had a long talk with Leslie myself a couple days after I got home. I needed to know things you couldn't tell me, Kelley. I hope you're not angry at me for that.

"Anyway, Leslie told me how she visited your school and brought things with her—some slides, a face mask, a big doll, one of those gloves. She explained everything and let the kids ask questions. So they would understand. When you returned in the fall."

Kelley couldn't believe it. Leslie had been in her school?

"Why didn't anyone tell me?"

"They didn't know how you'd take it, I guess. Mom was reluctant to say anything. There were so many other things for you to deal with."

Numbed by the news, Kelley set her spoon down and took her hands from the table. So the kids at school knew. They had *seen* the mask. Even Daniel!

Kelley tried to envision her classmates gathered around Leslie, listening, raising their hands to ask questions. *How long will she have to wear it? Even when she eats? Will she have scars? What does she look like?*

"Leslie said a lot of the kids wanted to know how they could help," Leah went on. "She told them there wasn't much they could do right then except to keep you in their prayers and maybe write a note."

A note. That's why so many of her classmates had written to her the last week of school. Haughtily, she had dropped their unopened letters into a basket. She hadn't read a single one. She hadn't even given them a chance! She had judged them as superficially as she feared they would judge her.

"Ah! *La salade!*" Leah exclaimed as the waiter arrived with two plates.

Kelley's cheeks grew warm with emotion and regret. She fumbled with her napkin. *The kids in class were reaching out to her. So maybe they wouldn't be so mean. Now that they understood. She should at least give them a chance. Give herself a chance.*

A tiny loaf of hot herbed bread arrived next, then crab cakes with sautéed zucchini and almonds. The café was filling with people. Kelley looked back to Leah, who smiled and was holding out a slice of warm, buttered bread.

When they had finished eating, Kelley put the mask back on and pulled her hair out from beneath the Velcro straps. Weird, but while she waited for Leah to pay the check she thought of Christine again. Christine with no fingers on her left hand, arms thrust out in front of her, diving into a pool and going all out for first place.

Leah handed Kelley her crutches.

It was only 2:00 P.M., Kelley saw, glancing at her watch. "Do we have time for one more floor?" she asked.

# twenty-two

"I REALLY WANT TO THANK you," Kelley said when Leah stopped the car at home. "It was fun. Maybe next week we could go somewhere else."

"The mall?" Leah suggested.

Kelley hesitated. "Maybe," she said, still wary of all the people who would be there. On the other hand, she thought, she had these earrings she was eager to wear. "I'd sort of like to get my ears pierced again. There's a store there that does it—"

"Oh, I know—Claire's! That's where I got mine done."

"Really? I didn't know Claire's has been there that long."

"Hey, watch it. I'm not *that* old." Leah shook her finger at Kelley, then grabbed her hand. "I think we should do it. Today the museum, tomorrow the mall!"

"Let me think about it," Kelley said.

Leah helped her out of the car and up the steps into the kitchen, where Tigger was waiting on the counter inside the door.

"You know you're not supposed to be up here," Kelley scolded, setting her crutches against the wall.

"Hey, I want you to think about this, too," Leah said, coming in behind her. "I had an idea. Mike came into the shop the other day. Mike, the stockbroker?"

Kelley nodded. Mike was the man who liked her mother.

"He knew who I was," Leah said, "and started asking me about Mom. You know? I think he still likes her, Kel. And he's a *really nice guy!*"

Leah put a gallon of milk they had picked up at the store into the refrigerator. "Anyway, I got to thinking," she went on. "Why don't I ask Mom if I can have someone to dinner one night? I'll tell her it's someone I met at the gift shop. I don't have to tell her exactly *who.*"

Kelley wasn't sure how her mother would react, but it sounded like a brave and exciting thing to do. She nodded. "Yeah! Let's do it."

"Good! I'll work out the details." She winked at Kelley. "Well, I'm going straight on to work, then. You're sure you'll be okay?"

Kelley nodded. "Mom will be home soon."

After Leah left, Kelley closed the door, scooped up her cat, and suddenly realized how tired her leg was from all the walking. She set Tigger down and used the crutches to walk into the living room. Except for the faint hum of the air-conditioning and the ticking of the clock on the mantel, it was silent in the house. Soft spears of late afternoon light fell through the blinds that covered the glass doors and windows facing west.

Kelley sat on the couch and picked up the TV guide, then set it back down. There was something eerie about the silence. She pushed herself back up and went to her mother's office to see if there were any messages on the answering machine.

Today's mail was piled on the desk and her mother's briefcase was on the floor. She was home? Kelley sat down and, through the window over the desk, could see someone—her mother—standing down on the dock. She must have gotten a ride home early. Maybe they could do something together—go somewhere, Kelley thought, feeling quite brave. On second thought, she realized, she didn't have the energy.

She scooped up the mail and slumped back in the big swivel chair. There was a moose postcard from Liesel, who wrote that she would be home in a few days. Alison was due back, too. Kelley couldn't wait to see them.

An envelope in the pile of mail caught her eye. It was from her mother's attorney, Anthony Brady. She recognized his name. He had come to the hospital once to talk to Kelley about what she remembered. The envelope had already been opened. Curious, she pulled out the papers inside.

*Dear Marjorie—As you know, I have been discussing your accident with the attorney for Quentin Hall. They now have filed a suit against you. This is a standard development and a way for Mr. Hall to try to recover money for his damages. Apparently, there was a witness. I'm hopeful insurance will cover everything, but I'm enclosing a copy of the complaint. . . .*

Kelley's heart pounded. She sat up and lifted the attorney's letter. Underneath was a copy of the lawsuit filed in Queen Anne's County Circuit Court.

*Plaintiff Quentin Hall,* she read silently, *by and through his undersigned attorneys, hereby sues Defendant Marjorie Hanson Brennan for negligence and states the following in support. On April 29 Ms. Brennan was the owner and operator of a station wagon traveling east off the exit ramp to Route 8 from U.S. Route 50. At approximately 8:00 P.M., while operating her car, she failed to stop for a plainly visible red light at the intersection of Route 8. . . .*

*As a result of the accident, Mr. Hall has suffered from double vision and a broken collarbone. . . . Mr. Hall has been unable to work. . . . Mr. Hall's truck suffered severe damage on the driver's side . . . lost wages.*

"I don't believe this," she said out loud. "She *did* run the red light. She *knows.*"

Kelley skimmed over several paragraphs to find out what they wanted, how much money was involved.

*Wherefore, Quentin Hall asks this honorable Court to find Marjorie Hanson Brennan liable for negligence and award him One Hundred Thousand Dollars ($100,000) for damages.*

Glancing out the window, Kelley saw her mother starting up the hill.

Had her mother known it all along? Why hadn't she

said anything? Hastily, Kelley stuffed the papers back in the envelope, grabbed her crutches, and stood up.

They met in the living room, and Kelley could see right away the strain on her mother's tired face.

"Kelley!" she said, closing the glass door to the deck. "You're back! Did you have a good time?"

Kelley nodded. "We did."

Her mother had on soft woven shoes and a flowery shift. Her hair was loose, but Kelley could see where she had raked it back with her fingers.

She came over to give Kelley a hug, and Kelley hugged her back.

"I do need to sit down, though," Kelley said.

Her mother sat in a chair opposite Kelley on the sofa. "Well, tell me about it," she said with apparent effort. "How'd you like the museum?"

Kelley sighed. She couldn't pretend for very long. "Everything went okay. But—why are you home? I thought you had appointments."

Her mother pressed her hands together. "I canceled them," she said.

She paused, so Kelley asked, "Why?"

Her mother looked up at her. "Because I need to talk to you," she said. "I have something I must tell you. Something I've needed to tell you for a long time."

Kelley knew she could have jumped in and saved her the trouble, but somehow she needed to hear her mother say it. It hurt, but she waited for her mother to find the words.

"Kelley," she began, slowly lifting her eyes. "It was my fault."

She did not have to say exactly what, because they both knew.

"I know," Kelley said.

"You do?"

Kelley nodded. "I've known ever since the hospital. I remembered."

Her mother covered her mouth. "Oh, Kelley! What I've done—"

Kelley said nothing, just sat, waiting, unsure of how she felt.

With effort, her mother regained her composure, and, although her eyes quickly filled with tears, she spoke calmly.

"I was in a rush," she began, "in a rush to get home because people were waiting to see the house."

She paused. "When I ran the red light, Kelley, do you know what I was thinking?"

Kelley stared at her.

"I was thinking that if I got there first, ahead of those people, that I'd have time to vacuum the living-room rug and empty the wastebasket in the bathroom."

Kelley had to look away.

"I don't know where to begin to tell you how sorry I am, Kelley. How I will always be sorry for changing your life that night. For putting you through all that . . . that pain." Her voice broke.

Kelley's throat grew tight, and tears pooled in her eyes, too.

"Why didn't you tell me before?" Kelley asked. "Why did you wait so long?"

Her mother shook her head. "I was afraid," she said. "Afraid that you wouldn't have anything to do with me. I had nightmares about it. I couldn't sleep. I didn't know what to do! I started seeing a psychologist."

"A psychologist? Is that the Dr. Hoffberg on the answering machine?"

"Lillian Hoffberg, yes. She's helping me, Kelley, to deal with this horrible thing that I've done. I told her, I said, 'Sometimes I feel as though I don't even have a right to live because of what I've done.' "

It was a startling thought. Despite everything, Kelley couldn't imagine not having her mother here. "It was an accident," she murmured.

"Yes. Yes it was," her mother said. "But it was an accident that didn't need to happen. If, for once in my life— *once in my life*—I had slowed down to see what was really important, this never would have happened!

"But I didn't, Kelley, and this is the price I will pay for the rest of my life. My beautiful little girl . . ." She began to cry. "Oh, Kelley, I can't believe I did this . . . that I ruined your life."

Kelley sat up. "You did *not* ruin my life," she argued.

"No, no, I didn't mean that," her mother scrambled. "Of course not. You have so much to offer, Kelley. It's just that—well, look at you. I mean, you'll never be the same." She put a hand over her face.

"You're wrong," she said angrily. "Look at me, Mom. *Look!*"

When her mother brought her hand down, Kelley had her mask off.

"I'm still Kelley. I am still the same Kelley that I always was. I may look different, but I'm still here."

Her mother remained still, holding both her hands close to her chest.

"I am more than just a bunch of scars!" Kelley declared. And, as she said it, she could feel the ripping pain as Kelley on the inside struggled to burst through and become Kelley on the outside once again.

"Of course you are, sweetie—"

"Then don't say you ruined my life!" Kelley hollered.

Her mother shook her head and shrank back. "I won't. I won't ever say it again."

Kelley sighed and felt an odd but welcome sense of peace.

"There's more," her mother ventured quietly. "There's been a lawsuit."

"I know. I saw the letter from your attorney." Kelley's voice dropped. "I read it."

"So everything will be in the papers. I'm having a hard enough time concentrating at work, being cheerful, and so forth. Everyone there is wonderful. I'm sure they'll be supportive. But I honestly don't know how much longer I can do that job. If I lose it, I'll have to start all over again. We'll have to sell this house for sure, just to keep up."

Kelley shrugged. "So we sell the house," she said. "People move all the time. We could move somewhere simpler. Closer to school maybe."

"School? But Leah said you didn't want to go back. She's been looking into home schooling—"

"I'm not as scared as I was," Kelley said. "I know Alison and Liesel will stand by me. I can give it a try."

Astonished, her mother listened.

"The house doesn't matter," Kelley said. "What matters is that we have each other—you and me and Leah."

"Oh, Kelley, I don't want you to hate me."

Kelley dropped her eyes and shook her head slowly. "I don't hate you," she said softly, "and I do need you." Her bottom lip trembled as she looked up. "You're my mom."

It was very strange to be thinking this, but that silly little game she and her mother used to play—turning a scribble into a picture—flashed into her mind. Here was the biggest, darkest scribble of all time, Kelley was thinking, and she had transformed it into a picture.

The next morning, Kelley awoke early to the raspy sound of her blue heron. She pushed the window up so she could hear him better. She would miss him if they left Loblolly Point, but in some ways, Kelley was excited about a move into town.

She took a deep breath of the fresh morning air and went to her bureau, where, in one quick motion, she whipped off the towel that covered the mirror. She fixed a ponytail with her clean, wet hair, put her mask on, and went to the kitchen, where her mother was already busy penciling in plans for the day. Leah sat at the table peeling an orange.

Kelley and her mother were going to spend the day together, riding around, deciding in which neighborhoods they would look for a new home, and where they might board EO. But there was one other thing they were going to do first.

"Good morning," her mother said, pushing aside the daily organizer. "You look nice."

"And very sexy," Leah added.

"It's just jeans," Kelley said. But the jeans were clean and the long-sleeved blue T-shirt was satin-edged and new.

"I love the top," Leah said.

Kelley looked down at it. "Ummm. Me, too. I bought it for the May Day Dance, but I never got to wear it."

Leah and her mother watched her.

"I forgot how much I loved it," Kelley said. She looked at her sister and her mother. "So what's for breakfast?"

Kelley's mother stood and lifted a bowl in front of her. "Waffles," she said, pouring batter onto the hot waffle iron.

Leah jumped up to pull out a chair for Kelley.

"What time did Daniel say to be there?" Kelley's mother asked.

"Nine o'clock," Kelley said.

"I am so jealous. I wish I could go, too," Leah said, making a face as she went back to work on her orange. "I said I'd fill in this morning at the gift shop."

"We've got plenty of time, Kelley," her mother said. "You won't be late, so don't worry."

Kelley laughed a little. "Being late is *not* what I'm worried about."

Leah gave her a sympathetic smile and Kelley's mother came over to give her a hug. "You'll be fine," her mother assured her.

There were only two cars parked in front of the Islander Hardware Store when they arrived. While Kelley waited for her mother to come around and help her out, she stared at the storefront and saw people moving around inside.

She could probably walk without the crutches today, but her mother had insisted. "Look how tired you got yesterday hiking all over Baltimore." So Kelley fixed the crutches under her arms and used them to make the short trip easier.

Mr. Banker was there.

So was Daniel. He was standing with a camera around his neck and a slight, tentative grin on his face.

"Well. Hell-o there," Mr. Banker said. "It's good to see you, Kelley."

Kelley nodded, embarrassed—scared now because Daniel hadn't said anything, and she didn't have the courage to look at him for very long.

Mr. Banker introduced himself to Kelley's mother and they shook hands.

"Kelley, I'm really glad you came," Daniel said.

Kelley raised her eyes and took in Daniel's familiar,

terrific smile. He had a great tan and his hair was long, but otherwise he hadn't changed a bit.

"I brought my Nikon," he said, holding up his camera. "Do you know there are over two hundred terns up there?"

Kelley nodded shyly. "I saw them once, a couple weeks ago. I didn't know how many, though."

"Shall we get started?" Mr. Banker asked, rubbing his hands together.

They moved to the stairs at the back of the store, where Kelley handed the crutches to her mother. "There's a handrail. I can make it up," she said.

Her mother didn't argue. She took the crutches and gave Kelley her Orioles hat and her sketch pad. There was a pencil in Kelley's pocket.

Kelley put the baseball cap on, and when she turned around, Daniel was waiting.

"Here," he said, taking her left hand. "I'll help you."

The stairway was narrow and dark, but Daniel's hand was warm and strong. Kelley had to take the stairs slowly, but she could have climbed forever, she was thinking. Her heart pounded with excitement as they stepped out into the bright sun on the flat, gravelly rooftop.

The terns immediately scattered. Dozens of them wheeled noisily above.

"Isn't it great?" Daniel asked, beaming at the spectacle. He squeezed her hand a little and let go of it so he could start taking pictures.

Kelley bit her lip and hugged her sketch pad, trying

196

hard to hold in the emotion because yes, indeed, when you stopped to look, it was beautiful. Not only because the little birds were flying safely beyond the edges that once defined their lives, but so was Kelley.

There was a path out into the world for Kelley Anne Brennan, a path that led to a place. She would follow that path, and when the going got rough, as surely it would, she would remind herself of what she had, and who she was, inside and out. Anything was possible now. And here to prove it was one girl's face, behind a mask, smiling back at the world.

**Priscilla Cummings** is the author of several books for children, including the novel *Autumn Journey*. A former newspaper reporter and magazine writer, Ms. Cummings first came to understand the enormous courage that burn victims and their caregivers must develop while she was researching a story.